The

AKIMBO

Adventures

The
AKIMBO
Adventures

ALEXANDER
McCALL SMITH

EGMONT

EGMONT

We bring stories to life

Akimbo and the Elephants
First published in Great Britain in 1990
Akimbo and the Lions
First published in Great Britain in 1992
Akimbo and the Crocodile Man
First published in Great Britain in 1993

First published in ebook format as *The Akimbo Adventures* 2013
This edition first published 2015 by Egmont UK Limited
The Yellow Building, 1 Nicholas Road, London W11 4AN

ISBN 978 1 4052 6534 8

A CIP catalogue record for this title is available from the British Library

Printed and bound in Great Britain by the CPI Group

54024/1

Contents

Akimbo and the Elephants

Akimbo and the Lions

Akimbo and the Crocodile Man

AKIMBO
AND THE
ELEPHANTS

This book is for Alan
and Barbara Hannah,
and for Jeremy and Kathryn

Contents

Akimbo's wish   1

Father elephant   9

Stolen ivory   19

The enemy   29

The hunt   39

Escape   53

Rhino charge   63

Elephants in danger   79

Akimbo's wish

Imagine living in the heart of Africa. Imagine living in a place where the sun rises each morning over blue mountains and great plains with grass that grows taller than a man. Imagine living in a place where there are still elephants.

Akimbo lived in such a place, on the edge of a large game reserve in Africa. This was a place where wild animals could live in safety. On its plains there were great herds of antelope and zebra. In the forests and in the

1

rocky hills there were leopards and baboons. And, of course, there were the great elephants, who roamed slowly across the grasslands and among the trees.

Akimbo's father worked here. Sometimes he drove trucks; sometimes he manned the radio or helped to repair the trucks. There was always something to do.

If Akimbo was lucky, his father would occasionally take him with him to work. Akimbo loved to go with the men when they went off deep into the reserve. They might have to mend a game fence or rescue a broken-down truck, or it might just be a routine patrol through the forest to check up on the animals.

Sometimes on these trips, they would see something exciting.

'Look over there,' his father would say.

'Don't make a noise. Just look over there.'

And Akimbo would follow his father's gaze and see some wild creature eating, or resting, or crouching in wait for its prey.

One day, when they were walking through the forest together, Akimbo's father suddenly seized his arm and whispered to him to be still.

'What is it?' Akimbo made his voice as soft as he could manage.

'Walk backwards. Very slowly. Go back the way we came.'

It was only as he began to inch back, that Akimbo realised what had happened. There in a clearing not far away were two leopards. One of them, sensing that something was happening, had risen to its feet and was sniffing at the air. The other was still sleeping.

Luckily, the wind was blowing in the wrong direction, or the leopard would have smelled their presence. If that had happened, then they would have been in even greater danger.

'That was close,' his father said, once they had got away. 'I don't like to think what would have happened if I hadn't noticed them in time.'

It was not leopards, or even lions, that Akimbo liked to watch. He loved the elephants best of all. You had to keep clear of them, too, but they seemed more gentle than many of the other creatures. Akimbo loved their vast, lumbering shapes. He loved the way they moved their trunks slowly, this way and that, as they plodded across the plains between the stretches of

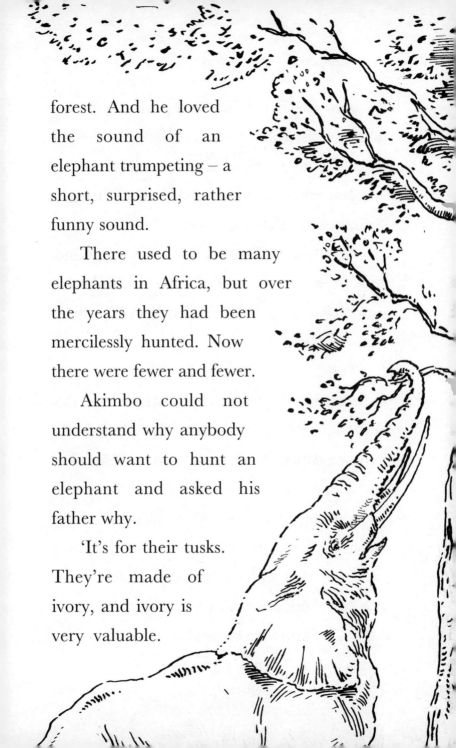

forest. And he loved the sound of an elephant trumpeting – a short, surprised, rather funny sound.

There used to be many elephants in Africa, but over the years they had been mercilessly hunted. Now there were fewer and fewer.

Akimbo could not understand why anybody should want to hunt an elephant and asked his father why.

'It's for their tusks. They're made of ivory, and ivory is very valuable.

It's used for ornaments and jewellery. Some rich people collect it and like to show off elephant tusks carved into fancy shapes.'

'But it's so cruel,' said Akimbo. 'I'm glad it doesn't happen any more.'

Akimbo's father was silent for a moment.

'I'm afraid it does still happen. There are still people who hunt elephants – even here in the reserve.'

'Can't you stop them?' he asked.

Akimbo's father shook his head. 'It's very difficult. The reserve stretches for almost a hundred miles. We can't keep an eye on all of it all the time.'

Akimbo was silent. The thought of the elephants being hunted for their tusks made him seethe with anger. He wondered whether there would come a day when all the elephants in Africa were destroyed. Then all that we would have to remember them by would be photographs and, of course, the ivory from their tusks. The reserves would be empty then, and the sight of the elephants crossing the plains would be nothing but a memory.

'I don't want that to happen,' Akimbo said to himself. 'I want the elephants to stay.'

Father elephant

A few weeks later, Akimbo was to be reminded of what his father had said about the poachers.

'We have to go out to check up on a water hole,' his father said. 'Do you want to come with us?'

'Yes,' said Akimbo eagerly.

'It'll be a rough ride,' his father warned him. 'There isn't even a track for much of the way.'

'I don't mind. I know how to hang on.'

9

Akimbo's father was right. It was not an easy journey, and it was very hot as well. At noon the sun burned down unmercifully, and it was unbearably hot in the truck cabin. Akimbo wiped the sweat off his face and drank great gulps of water from the water bottles, but he did not complain once.

They had to travel slowly, as there were rocks and potholes which could easily damage the truck if they came upon them too quickly. Every now and then, a concealed rock would scrape against the bottom of the truck with a painful, jarring sound, and everybody inside would wince. But no damage was done, and they continued their journey.

During the hot hours of midday, few animals will venture out of the shade of the trees and the undergrowth. But Akimbo saw a small herd of zebra cantering off to safety, throwing up a cloud of dust behind them.

Then, quite suddenly, one of the men in the back of the truck hit his fist on the top of the roof and pointed off to the left. Akimbo's father brought the vehicle to a halt.

'What is it?' he called out.

The man leaned over into the cabin.

'Vultures. Flocks of them.'

The eyes of all the others followed the man's gaze. Akimbo saw nothing at first, but when he craned his neck he saw the birds circling in the hot, still air. Even from this distance, he could tell that there were lots of them, and so he knew that something big was attracting their attention.

Akimbo's father turned to one of the other men.

'Do you think the lions finished a meal?'

The other man looked thoughtful. 'Maybe. But there are rather a lot of vultures for that. Don't you think we should go and take a look?'

Akimbo's father agreed. Then, swinging the truck off to the left, he steered in the direction of the circling birds. After a bumpy ride of fifteen minutes they were there and they saw the sad sight which they had all secretly been dreading.

The elephant lay on its side, where it had fallen. As the truck approached, four or five vultures flapped up into the air, angry at the disturbance of their feeding. Akimbo's father looked furious as he drew the truck to a halt. Without speaking, he opened his door and strode off to stand beside the fallen elephant.

Akimbo stayed where he was. He could not bear to look at the great creature. He knew that the elephant had been destroyed so that its tusks could be stolen.

Akimbo looked away. There was a group of trees nearby and as Akimbo looked towards it he noticed movement. Then, a little way away, the vegetation moved.

Akimbo strained his eyes to try to see more. He was sure an animal was there, but it was difficult to see through the thick covering of leaves and branches. He hoped it was not a buffalo, which could be dangerous.

There was another movement, and this time Akimbo was looking in the right place. Quickly opening the door of the truck cabin, Akimbo leapt out and ran to where his father and the other men were standing.

'Look!' he cried out. 'Look over there.'

The men spun round. As they did so, the baby elephant broke cover. It took a few steps and then stopped, as if uncertain what to do. It raised its trunk and sniffed at the air. Then it dropped its trunk and stood quite still. Akimbo noticed that it had a torn right ear.

'It's her calf,' said his father. 'It's very young.'

They stared at the calf for a few moments.

The tiny elephant was obviously confused. It saw its mother lying motionless on the ground, and it wanted to join her. At the same time, its instinct told it to keep away from the intruding men.

'Can we look after it?' Akimbo asked.

Akimbo's father shook his head. 'No. The herd will pick it up. If we leave it here, another cow elephant will come for it.'

'But it's so small. Can't we take it back to the compound and look after it?'

'It will be all right,' said Akimbo's father. 'It's best not to interfere.'

They began to walk back to the truck. At a distance, the little elephant watched them go, withdrawing slightly as they moved. When the engine started, Akimbo saw it run back to the shelter of the trees.

'Goodbye,' Akimbo muttered under his

breath. 'Good luck.'

The truck turned away. Akimbo took one last glance back, and saw that the vultures, which had been circling high in the sky, had now dropped lower.

Stolen ivory

Over the next few days, Akimbo found himself thinking more and more about the baby elephant. He wondered whether it had been picked up by another member of the herd, or whether it had been left to die. Had the poachers destroyed two elephants in their cruel and greedy hunt for ivory?

He knew that his father and the other game rangers were doing their best to stop the hunters, but they seemed unable to deal with them.

'If I were in charge,' he said to himself, 'I'd catch them and teach them a lesson. If nobody else will, then I'm going to stop them.'

He thought about this. There was no reason why the poachers should get away with it. Perhaps there was something he could do, after all.

'Where do the poachers come from?' he asked his father one evening.

His father shrugged his shoulders. 'From all over the place. But we know that there's one gang in the village nearby. We can't prove it, but we think they're doing it.'

'What do they do with the tusks?' Akimbo asked.

His father sighed. 'They hide them. Traders come up from the towns and buy them from them. Then they smuggle the tusks back to town and that's where they're carved. They make them into necklaces and ornaments.'

'But don't you ever catch any of them?'

'Sometimes. Then we hand them over to the police. But the poachers are cunning, and clever as well.'

Akimbo turned away. 'I'm clever too,' he muttered under his breath. 'And I'm sure I can be as cunning as they are.'

'What was that?' his father asked.

'Nothing,' Akimbo replied. But he had declared war on the poachers the moment he saw that baby elephant waiting in vain for its mother to get up.

Akimbo knew that it would be impossible for him to do anything about the poachers in the reserve itself. The poaching gangs travelled by night, and were armed. Then they struck quickly and as quietly as possible, before fading away into the bush again. Every so often, the rangers picked up their tracks and pursued them, but usually they were too late.

He thought of different plans, but none of them seemed likely to work. If there was no point in his waiting for the poachers, why not go to the village and find them? That was the way to get the proof he would need to stop them.

At the edge of the rangers' camp there was a storeroom. Akimbo had been inside only once or twice, as it was always kept locked, and his father rarely went there. In it were the things which the rangers confiscated from poachers when they managed to find them.

It was a grim collection. There were cruel barbed-wire traps, designed to tighten like a noose around an animal's leg when it stepped into the concealed circle of wire. There were rifles, spears and ammunition belts. But what was saddest of all were the parts of animals which had been caught by the poachers. As well as horns and skins, there were the most sought-after trophies of all, the tusks of elephants.

Many of these things were kept to show to visitors, so that they could see what the poachers did. Some were also kept in the hope they would be needed as evidence once the poachers were caught. But that seemed to happen so rarely that the tusks and the traps just gathered more and more dust.

That night, at a time when the rest of the camp was asleep, Akimbo slipped out of his room and made his way across the compound towards the storeroom. In the moonlight he could make out the shape of the storeroom against the night sky. He paused in the shadows for a few moments, to check that nobody was about, and then he

darted along the path to stand in front of the storeroom door.

His father's bunch of keys was heavy in his pocket. He had slipped it out of the pocket of his father's working tunic while his parents were busy in the kitchen. He had felt bad about that, but he told himself that he was not stealing anything for himself.

Now he tried each key in the storeroom lock. It was a slow business. In spite of the moonlight, there was still not enough light to see clearly, and it was difficult to keep those keys he had already used from being jumbled up with those which he had yet to try.

At one point he dropped the whole bunch, and it made a loud, jangly noise, but nobody woke up.

At last the lock moved, and with a final twist the bolt slid home. Akimbo pushed open the door and wrinkled his nose as he smelled the familiar, rotten odour of the uncured skins. But it was not skins he had come for. There, in a corner, was a small elephant tusk, which had been roughly sawn in two. Akimbo picked this up, checked that it was not too heavy to carry, and took it out of the storeroom. He took off its label. Then, locking the door again, he crept away, just like a poacher making off with his load of stolen ivory.

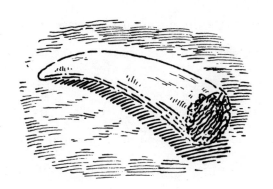

The enemy

'I'd like to go to the village,' Akimbo told his parents the following morning.

Akimbo's father seemed surprised.

'Why? There's nothing for you to do there.'

'There's Mato. I haven't seen him for a long time. I'd like to see him. Last time I was there his aunt said that I could stay with them for a few days.'

His father shrugged his shoulders, looking at Akimbo's mother.

'If you want to go, I suppose you can,' she said. 'You'll have to walk there, though. It'll take three hours – maybe more. And don't be any trouble for Mato's aunt.'

Again Akimbo felt bad. He did not like to lie to his parents, but if he told them of his plan he was sure that they would prevent him from trying it out. And if that happened, then nobody would ever stop the poachers, and the hunting of the elephants would go on and on.

As his father had warned him, the walk was not easy. And, carrying a chunk of ivory in a sack over his shoulder, Akimbo found it even more difficult than he had imagined. Every few minutes he had to stop and rest, sliding the sack off his shoulder and waiting for his tired arm muscles to recover. Then he

would heave the sack up again and continue his walk, keeping away from the main path to avoid meeting anybody.

At last the village was in sight. Akimbo did not go straight in, but looked around in the bush for a hiding place. Eventually he found an old termite hole. He stuffed the sack in it and placed a few dead branches over the top. It was the perfect place.

Once in the village, he went straight to Mato's house. Mato lived with his aunt. She was a nurse and ran the small clinic at the edge of the village. Mato was surprised to see Akimbo, but pleased, and took him in for a cup of water in the kitchen.

'I need your help,' said Akimbo to his friend. 'I want to find somebody who will buy some ivory from me.'

Mato's eyes opened wide with surprise.

'But where did you get it?' he stuttered. 'Did you steal it?'

Akimbo shook his head. Then, swearing his friend to secrecy, he told him his plan. Mato thought for a while and then he gave him his opinion.

'It won't work,' he said flatly. 'You'll just

get into trouble. That's all that will happen.'

Akimbo shook his head.

'I'm ready to take that risk.'

So Mato, rather reluctantly, told Akimbo about a man in the village whom everyone thought was dishonest.

'If I had something stolen which I wanted to sell,' he said, 'I'd go to him. He's called Matimba, and I can show you where he lives. But I'm not going into his house. You'll have to go in on your own.'

Matimba was not there the first time that Akimbo went to the house. When he called an hour later, though, he was told to wait at the back door. After ten minutes or so the door opened and a stout man with a beard looked out.

'Yes,' he said, his voice curt and suspicious.

'I would like to speak to you,' Akimbo said politely.

'Then speak,' snapped Matimba.

Akimbo looked over his shoulder.

'I have something to sell. I thought you might like it.'

Matimba laughed. '*You* sell something to *me*?'

Akimbo ignored the laughter.

'Yes. Here it is.'

When he saw the ivory tusk sticking out of the top of Akimbo's sack, Matimba stopped laughing.

'Come inside. And bring that with you.'

Inside the house, Akimbo was told to sit on a chair while Matimba examined the tusk. He looked at it under the light, sniffed it, and rubbed at it with his forefinger. Then he laid it down on a table and stared at Akimbo.

'Where did you get this?' he asked.

'I found it,' said Akimbo. 'I found a whole lot of tusks. And some rhino horns.'

At the mention of rhino horns, Matimba narrowed his eyes. These horns were much in demand among smugglers, and could fetch very high prices on the coast. If this boy has really got some, Matimba thought, I could get them off him for next to nothing.

'Where did you find them?'

'In a hiding place near a river. I think they must have been hidden there by a poacher who got caught and couldn't come back for them.'

Matimba nodded. This sort of thing did happen, and now this innocent boy had stumbled across a fortune. He looked at the tusk again. He would give him some money on the spot and promise him more if he took him to the rest.

'You did well to come to me. I can buy these things from you.'

Akimbo drew in his breath. Now was the time for him to make his demand.

'You can have them. I don't want money for them.'

Matimba was astonished. He looked again at the boy and wondered whether there was something wrong with him.

'All I want is to become an elephant hunter. If you let me go off with some poachers – to learn how they do it – I'll show you where I have hidden the tusks and horns.'

Matimba was silent. He stared at Akimbo for some time, wondering whether to trust him. Then his greed got the better of his caution. He granted Akimbo's wish. After all, boys thought poaching was exciting. Well, let him learn.

'You may go with my men,' he said.

Akimbo felt a great surge of excitement. Matimba had said 'my men'. He had found the head of a gang of poachers. His plan had worked – so far. The next stage was the really dangerous part.

The hunt

Matimba told Akimbo to come back the following night. He was to bring nothing with him and was to expect to be away for two or three days. The men would bring the food.

'I hope that you're strong enough,' he said dubiously. 'And I hope your parents won't come looking for you.'

Akimbo reassured him, but Matimba was no longer paying attention. He had picked up the tusk again, and was polishing at its surface with a cloth. Akimbo threw a last glance at it before he left the room He hoped that the loss of the tusk would not be noticed too soon. He would have to own up to taking it, but he only wanted to when his plan had been carried out. If it failed, then he did not look forward to confessing that he had given the tusk to the head of a poaching gang.

Mato was still worried. As they lay side by side on their sleeping mats, Mato told Akimbo: 'You're crazy. Go straight home and tell your father what you've done.'

Akimbo told him about how they had found the baby elephant, waiting for its mother.

'We can't let all the elephants of Africa be destroyed. I must do something for them.'

Mato was silent at the end of Akimbo's story.

'All right. I suppose I should say good luck.'

'Thank you,' said Akimbo. Then, feeling tired after the day's long walk, he drifted off to sleep, not hearing the sound of the village dogs barking, or the whine of the crickets outside. Mato stayed awake a little longer, worrying about his friend, but at last he, too, fell asleep.

The next day dragged past with a painful slowness. At last, as the sun began to sink below the hills, Akimbo knew that it was time

for him to go to Matimba's house. He was
the only person there to begin with, but a
little while later several men arrived. They
looked suspiciously at Akimbo, and spoke in
lowered voices to Matimba. After that, they
appeared to accept Akimbo's presence.

There were five men in the group. The
leader was a short man, who walked with a
limp. He gave orders to the others, who
obeyed him quickly and without question.
When the time came to leave, he told
Akimbo to walk immediately behind him

and not to speak once they set off.

'Keep quiet all the time. Do exactly as I tell you and you'll be all right. Understand?'

Akimbo nodded. The other men were ready now, and they slipped away from the village, following a path which led through the thick grass towards the hills in the distance. Over those hills lay the reserve, and deep in the reserve were the forests where the elephants lived. They were on their way.

They walked all night. Akimbo was used to walking long distances, but the speed with which the men travelled wore him out. He had to keep up, even though his feet were sore and he longed to lie down in the grass and go to sleep.

By the time the sun rose, they had already crossed into the reserve. Now that it was light, they moved cautiously, keeping to a route which took them through heavy vegetation. Akimbo wondered how long they could keep walking all day as well as all night. When could they sleep?

Suddenly the leader gestured with his hand and the men stopped.

'We'll rest here,' he said quietly. 'Find places to sleep. We'll move again tonight.'

Akimbo dropped to the ground underneath the cover of a small thorn bush. The ground was hard but he was so tired that it was more welcome to him than the softest bed. He closed his eyes against the glare of the day and was asleep within seconds.

He felt the hand of one of the men on his shoulder.

'Time to go,' a voice whispered. 'We're leaving.'

Akimbo sat up. His body felt sore from sleeping on the ground, and his throat was parched. One of the men gave him a drink of water from a bottle he was carrying. Then he gave him a large piece of dried meat to eat as they walked. The meat was tough and difficult to chew, but Akimbo gnawed at it hungrily.

It was almost dark by the time they set off. They had to travel more slowly now, as the ground was rough and the grass was thick and high. Akimbo had no idea where they were, but he knew that they must be nearing the place where they might expect to find elephants, as he had seen the forests in the distance when they stopped that morning.

They disturbed several wild animals as they made their way. An antelope bounded off from a hollow immediately ahead of them, crashing through the undergrowth in panic. Another large animal was disturbed a little later, and they heard it charging away during the night. It could have been a rhinoceros, and this frightened Akimbo as he knew how dangerous rhinos could be.

They stopped to rest once or twice, and Akimbo found himself less exhausted than on the previous night. At last, towards dawn, they stopped altogether. They were now in heavily wooded land, and at any point they might see elephant. Akimbo assumed that now the hunt was on.

That morning, after resting for three or four hours, the group began to move slowly through the clumps of great trees which broke up the plain. One of the men was now acting as a tracker, and he had picked up the signs of elephant. From time to time he pointed at something on the ground and said something to the man with the limp, who nodded.

Suddenly the tracker stopped. The leader went up to him and crouched beside him. Akimbo and the other men crouched down too, waiting for a sign from the leader.

Akimbo saw the elephants at the edge

of the trees. They were moving slowly, browsing among the branches of the trees with their trunks, pulling down clumps of foliage. His heart stopped for a moment. There was a male elephant among them who had a very large pair of tusks – great, white sweeps of ivory. Akimbo knew that the poachers would be bound to go for him.

Suddenly two of the elephants turned to face them. There was a ripple of activity amongst the others, as the two large bulls flapped out their ears and lifted their trunks in the direction of the crouching men. Akimbo realised that the animals had got their scent and were now alarmed. And if they were alarmed, then they might charge.

The leader gestured to one of the other men, who ran up to him with a rifle. The elephant must have seen the movement, as he suddenly moved forwards several paces and let out a bellow. Behind him, the other elephants had moved for protection into the shadows of the trees.

Akimbo had never seen a charging elephant and he was not ready for the speed with which it moved. For a few moments he was frozen in terror, his eyes fixed on the great creature which was charging towards them. Then, quite suddenly, the elephant stopped. For a short while it stood still, its ears out, its body quivering, small eddies of dust about its feet, and then, without warning, it turned aside and moved back towards the herd.

As this was happening, the leader was fumbling with the rifle. By the time he had it to his shoulder, the elephants had disappeared into the thickness of the forest. Akimbo felt all the fear drain out of his body. They were safe. And so were the elephants – at least, for the time being.

Escape

The leader was clearly angry over what had happened. He called his men over to him and spoke sharply to them, pointing to where the herd had been to underline his words. They all knew that the elephants would move quickly, now that they had scented danger, and that it would be difficult to catch up with the herd.

For a few minutes the leader seemed uncertain what to do. Then he spoke. 'We'll follow them. I want to get those tusks.'

One of the men stepped forwards.

'But they're going west. There are rangers that way. It would be too dangerous. They might . . .'

The leader interrupted him abruptly.

'I want those tusks. If you're frightened, you can go home now.'

The man looked down.

'I'm not frightened.'

Akimbo listened. The information that they were going to travel west excited him. In that direction lay the ranger camp, and home, and this would make it easier for him to carry out his plan.

With the tracker in the front, his eyes glued to the ground, the line of poachers snaked its way through the thick savannah. Tracking elephants was much easier than tracking other animals, as elephants destroy so much as they make their way, but even so it took all the tracker's skill.

By late afternoon there was still no sign of the elephants and Akimbo wondered what they would do when darkness fell. It would be impossible then to follow the herd any further – and dangerous, too, as they could suddenly find themselves in the middle of the herd in the darkness, and they would stand no chance then.

When the light became too bad to go on, the leader called his men to a halt. Everybody was tense, weary, and thirsty, and they were pleased to be able to rest.

'We will spend the night here. At first light we can go on.'

'But we're too close to the ranger camp,' one of the others said. 'It's only one or two hours that way.'

Akimbo watched where the man pointed. Then, without bothering to hear the leader's answer, he walked off and lay beneath a nearby bush, curling up as if to sleep. The other men all settled themselves too, concealing themselves beneath branches or bushes, and soon anybody walking past would not have realised that five men and a boy were sleeping there.

The boy was not asleep. Although his bones ached with tiredness, Akimbo fought back the waves of drowsiness, and he struggled to keep his mind on what he had to do. At last, when he was sure that all the others were fast asleep, he crept out from underneath his

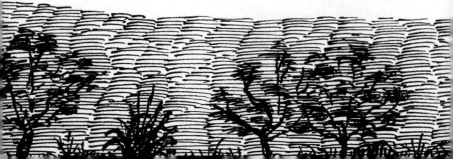

sheltering place.

Nobody moved. Nor did anybody stir as he began to move off in the direction of the ranger camp, which one of the men had pointed out.

'I hope he was right,' he said to himself. 'If he's not . . .' But Akimbo did not allow himself to think about that. For the moment he knew exactly what he had to do, and he concentrated all his energy on doing it.

It was more frightening than Akimbo could ever have imagined. The moon was behind cloud, and there was very little light. All that he could make out around him were large black shapes – the shapes of trees, bushes, rocks. Akimbo tried to fix his mind on some

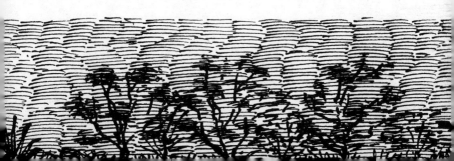

landmark in order to keep travelling in the right direction, but it was almost impossible to do this in the darkness. The shape which he aimed for would suddenly be lost, or would look different when he approached it, and there was no way of telling that he was not going round in one large circle.

'If I'm just going round and round I'll come back to where I started from and I'll

walk right into the poachers.'

After about fifteen minutes the cloud cleared and there was a little more light from the sky. Akimbo could now identify an object to aim for in the distance. He could also move faster, as he did not have to worry so much about the ground suddenly giving way over a cliff.

He broke into a run. It was painful to his tired legs, but he managed to push himself to do it. He scratched himself, of course, on thorn bushes and protruding twigs, but he did not mind that. All he wanted now was to reach the ranger camp and safety.

Suddenly Akimbo stopped. His heart was

pounding within him, his skin prickling with fear. Had his ears deceived him, or was it ... Yes. There it was again. It was a roar. Still quite distant, but unmistakably the roar of a lion.

Akimbo looked about him in panic. All he saw were the same dark shapes and shadows of the African night. Lions could be anywhere. They could be watching him at this moment. They could be crouched, ready to pounce.

He shook his head. He would not give up now. He would not look for the nearest tree and try to climb to safety. He had to get home.

Rhino charge

Moving as quietly as he could, Akimbo made his way through the thick scrub bush. It was difficult to travel quietly, though, unless he also went slowly. And if he went slowly, then that would make him more likely to be attacked.

He stopped for a moment and listened. The African night is never quiet. There was the sound of insects, a shrill screeching noise that never stopped. It was everywhere – behind him, around him, above him, and it was difficult to make out any other sound. Yet there it was. There was a sound which was different.

Akimbo took a deep breath. For a few seconds he felt like shouting out, in the hope that somebody might hear him. But he knew that there was nobody about and shouting could make his situation even worse. He turned round. Did the sound come from behind?

There was silence. Akimbo took another step, and then stopped again. He was sure that he had heard something.

'I'm being stalked. That means it's a lion, or maybe a leopard.'

The thought of the fierce animal behind him made his skin chill. He looked about for a tree, and saw one a few yards away in the darkness. 'I can climb that. It's not high, but

at least
it'll give me
some protection.'

Slowly he moved over to the tree and reached up for the first, lower branches. His arms were weak with fear, but he still felt strong enough to pull himself up off the ground. Then, just as he began to raise himself, he heard a crashing sound behind him. The fear made him let go, and he dropped down in a heap, the wind knocked out of him.

The crashing noise grew louder as the animal charged through the undergrowth. Akimbo tried to struggle to his feet, but his limbs would not respond. He was paralysed with fright.

The rhino moved with extraordinary speed. When Akimbo first saw it, it was a dark blur, heading straight towards him, and then in no more than a few seconds, it had shot past, thundering off beyond the tree.

Akimbo stayed quite immobile. As the rhino moved off, the crashing sound grew fainter, and, after a while, there was quiet again. Akimbo picked himself up and found, to his surprise, that he was quite unhurt. The rhino must have missed him by inches.

He started to walk again, dazed, overwhelmed by the closeness of his escape. He realised that he must have been following the rhino for a while and that they had both been equally surprised to find one another. When the rhino had eventually seen him, it had charged, but it had really only meant to get away.

Akimbo now felt all his fear leave him. He had survived a trip with poachers; he had survived a charging rhino. He felt strong now, and he knew that he could make it home.

Akimbo was to remember little of the few hours that followed. He walked quickly, and tried to keep going in a straight line. He whistled for a while, and he remembered bruising himself against a rock which was hidden in the grass. And then at last there was the supreme moment when he saw the lights away to his left, almost obscured by trees and not in the direction in which he would have expected them to be. Yet there was only one thing they could be – the lights of the ranger camp.

* * *

His parents were already asleep by the time he reached home. His father woke up at the sound of the door being opened and got out of bed to see his son stagger in from the night.

'Akimbo! What are you doing here?'

Akimbo took some time to catch his breath again. Then, when he could speak, he blurted out his message.

'There's a gang of poachers. They're in the reserve. They're after elephants.'

'How on earth do you know?'

Akimbo told him everything. As he spoke, he watched his father's eyes bulge with surprise.

'But what on earth made you do it?' his father asked, half in anger, half in astonishment.

Akimbo did not give him an answer.

'Look, Father, just believe me. They're there. I know where they are. I can take you there.'

Akimbo's father looked doubtful. Then he appeared to make up his mind. He told Akimbo to stay where he was while he went off to summon the head ranger. It was up to him to decide what should be done next.

The head ranger listened gravely to Akimbo's story. When it came to the description of how he had taken the ivory from the storeroom, he frowned and looked angry.

'You shouldn't have done that. You know that was stealing.'

'But I only wanted to help. I couldn't let the poachers get away with it.'

'That's not your job,' interrupted the head ranger. 'It's not up to you to stop them.'

Akimbo was silent. It was so unfair that the poachers could get away with their greed and cruelty and nobody could stop them. Then, when somebody did try, all he got himself into was trouble.

Akimbo looked at his father, silently appealing for help.

'He has more to say,' said his father quietly. 'I think you should hear him out.'

The head ranger nodded, still frowning, but when Akimbo told him of his meeting with Matimba he smiled and nodded, pleased at getting the first piece of firm evidence against a man whom he had long suspected.

At the end of Akimbo's tale, the head ranger rose to his feet and rubbed his hands together.

Akimbo waited anxiously.

'Thank you. Well done!'

And with those few words, Akimbo knew that everything would be all right. Or rather, it would be all right if they caught the poachers. If they didn't, then he was sure the blame would land fairly and squarely on himself.

The head ranger now gave orders for all the rangers to be woken. They had to be ready to leave the camp within an hour. They would travel on foot, he said, as the last thing he wanted was for the poachers to be given any warning of their presence.

'Can you manage to walk?' he asked Akimbo casually. 'You must be a bit tired.'

Akimbo swallowed. He doubted whether his legs could carry him any further, and the sight of his sleeping mat on the floor of their house had been almost too tempting. But he had started this, and he would have to finish it, even if he dropped in his shoes at the end of it all.

'I'm fine,' he replied cheerfully. 'I can do it.'

Ten rangers set off. They were all armed and equipped with everything they needed for a long hike. Akimbo walked beside the head ranger. Immediately behind him was

his father, who encouraged him quietly whenever he seemed to be flagging.

He had a good idea of the direction

from which he had come. He thought he recognised certain features – the tip of a hill, silhouetted black against the night sky, or a stretch of forest. But it all seemed so similar in the darkness and he knew that he could be quite wrong.

Just before dawn they stopped. As the light came up over the horizon and the sun painted the hills with red fire, Akimbo gazed around really puzzled.

'Do you recognise anything?' whispered the head ranger. 'Those trees over there? That hill?'

Akimbo shook his head.

'It seems so different. Everything seemed larger at night.'

The head ranger nodded.

'Don't worry. We'll just go forwards very slowly. If you see something familiar, tap me on the arm – don't speak.'

Slowly they made their way through the undergrowth. They were as quiet as they could be but there were twigs underfoot, which cracked as they trod on them. There were branches which swung back with a swishing sound when they bent them. One of the men coughed once or twice in spite of his efforts to suppress it.

Akimbo was sure they were lost. Should he tell the head ranger now that he had no idea where they were, rather than let them waste more time? But just as he was about to attract the head ranger's attention, he saw it.

There had been a cactus very close to where he had lain down and pretended to sleep. And now, he saw it again. It was definitely the same one. There was that missing branch and the piece that bent down instead of up.

He reached out to attract the head ranger's attention.

'That's it,' he whispered. 'That's where I was.' At a signal from the head ranger, all the rangers dropped to the ground. Then, half crawling and half running, they moved swiftly towards the cactus.

There was nothing – no sign of the poachers at all. The rangers poked around under the bushes. One came across an empty water bottle and held it up for the others to see. Another found a couple of burned-out matches and showed them to the head ranger.

It was now the turn of the ranger who was most skilled at tracking. He walked about the site where the men had camped that night until he was satisfied that he could work out which direction they had followed. Then, just as the poachers' own tracker had done, he set off, following the signs on the ground, stopping from time to time to peer closely at a footprint or a tuft of grass that had been flattened by somebody's boot.

'They're not far away,' he said to the head ranger. 'Nor are the elephants.'

Elephants in danger

As they set off along the tracks of the poachers, Akimbo wondered whether they would be in time. Sooner or later the poachers would catch up with the herd of elephants, and once they did that the fate of the elephant with the handsome tusks would be decided. Akimbo did not care so much if the poachers got away – although he wanted them to be caught – what really mattered to him was stopping them from killing that elephant.

And it seemed such a painfully slow chase!

'Can't we go faster?' Akimbo asked his father. 'If we don't hurry, they'll have got the tusks by the time we get anywhere near them.'

Akimbo's father patted his son on the shoulder.

'If we go too fast, we'll lose their trail. A tracker needs time.'

And so they inched their way onwards until the tracker suddenly held his hand up and everybody stood stock-still.

The head ranger moved quietly to the tracker's side.

'What is it?' he whispered.

The tracker pointed down to the ground.

'They're ten minutes ahead of us,' the tracker said. 'Look.'

He pointed down to the print of a man's boot in the soft sand. It was fresh and clear, and the tracker knew that it had been made only minutes before.

The head ranger signalled to his men to advance more carefully. Now they moved even more slowly, watching each footfall, avoiding stones and twigs and anything else that could give their presence away.

They had reached a place where the ground sloped sharply upwards. Ahead of them was the brow of a hill, and on the other side of that the ground sloped gently away to a plain.

The elephants were standing at the edge of a large clump of trees. They were foraging, reaching up with curling trunks to the high branches of trees, their ears fanning slowly to keep the flies away. There were several mother elephants with their young, and there, at the edge of the herd, was the magnificent male with his heavy tusks.

The sight of the elephants distracted the rangers. They had not expected to come across them so quickly, and at such close quarters. Nor had they expected to see the poachers so close to them, crouching only forty or fifty yards away.

Akimbo took in the scene in an instant. He saw the leader of the group of poachers half rise to his feet and bring the rifle to his shoulder, waiting for his opportunity to fire the shot that would bring his quarry crashing to the ground.

The seconds ticked past. Akimbo

looked about him. Nobody seemed to be doing anything, and he wondered whether the others had seen the leader. If they had not, then there was only one thing for him to do.

From his crouching position, Akimbo shot to his feet and launched himself forwards with a yell. He was aware of his father's cry of horror, but he lurched on, waving his arms, heading straight towards the herd of elephants.

There was a sudden rumpus of movement amongst the elephants. The smaller ones were quickly fussed away by their mothers while the great elephant with the tusks spun round to face the source of the disturbance. When the large elephant saw Akimbo, his ears flapped out and his trunk went up.

'No!' shouted Akimbo's father. 'Akimbo! Stop!'

The poachers burst out of their hiding places and stared at the boy. Their leader rose up and lowered his gun, looking around him in astonishment, uncertain what to do. Then he saw the rangers behind Akimbo and let out a cry of alarm.

The elephant was scenting the air. Akimbo had now dropped to the ground and was sheltering behind a small bush. The large elephant had lost sight of him now, and was peering in the direction from which he had been coming. He began to advance, trumpeting a warning as he did so.

Akimbo looked out from behind his hiding place. He could see the bulk of the elephant coming towards him but he was not sure if it could see him. He knew that he was in great danger, but for some reason he felt quite calm. His father's words came back to him. 'The best thing to do is to stay quite still.'

And he was right. The elephant took a few more steps forwards and then, no longer aware of the presence of the threat, he moved back to the herd and began to lead them off into the trees. As he did so, Akimbo stood up to get a better view of them. The elephant with the large tusks was encouraging the herd to move faster, pushing against one or two of the reluctant ones, urging the others on with swinging movements of his trunk.

Akimbo caught his breath. There were several baby elephants in the herd, and one of them he was sure he had seen before. Yes! There was no doubt about it. It was a baby

elephant with a tear in its right ear. So it had been found by the herd, and it was being looked after.

With the elephants dispersed, the rangers turned their attention to the poachers. The leader realised the gang were outnumbered and surrendered himself almost immediately. He was followed by all of his men. They glowered in anger at Akimbo. But Akimbo did not mind. The poachers could do him no harm now.

* * *

Akimbo's father seemed too shocked by what had happened to say much to his son on the way back to the camp. After a while, he managed to speak, still trembling.

'You were very, very lucky there. I thought the elephant would get you before we had time to do anything.'

'It almost did. But it was the only way I could warn it.'

'It was still no reason to take that risk. If you hadn't found that bush to drop behind, I don't know ...'

'But I *did* find it.'

The head ranger, who had been listening to them, now joined in.

'You were very brave. If it hadn't been for you, that elephant would have lost its life.'

Back at the camp the rangers arranged for the police to come out to collect the poachers and the head ranger had to pass on the information he had received about Matimba. He enjoyed doing this, as it would give him great pleasure to see Matimba arrested and his cruel trade in stolen ivory brought to an end.

But there was only one thing that Akimbo wanted to do. He lay down on his sleeping mat, feeling all the aching tiredness flow out of his weary limbs. Within seconds he was asleep.

He slept for almost twenty hours and at some point in that long sleep he dreamed. He dreamed of the elephants. He dreamed that he was out on the savannah, watching the elephant with the great tusks walk slowly through the waving, golden grass. And as it walked past, it turned and looked at him. This time it did not prepare to charge, but lifted its trunk, as if to salute Akimbo, its friend. And Akimbo raised his hand to it too, and then watched it walk slowly away.

AKIMBO
AND THE
LIONS

This book is for Victor
and Doreen

Contents

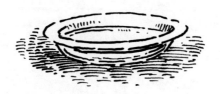

A lion problem   97

The trap   109

Lion!   121

Left behind   133

Becoming friends   147

Lion at school   159

Back to the wilds   169

A lion problem

There is a place in Africa where the hills give
way to great plains of grass. Zebra graze
here, and buffalo too, and if you are lucky,
you may also see lions. And at the water
holes in the morning, there are other animals
to be seen. There are giraffe, awkwardly
bending their long necks to the surface of the
water; warthogs, with their families,
scurrying in to quench their thirst while
nobody is looking; and many animals
besides. Akimbo, who lived on the edge of

this great game park, knew all the animals well, and their ways.

But now Akimbo was bored. His friends had gone away and it seemed that nothing at all was happening in the game park. His father was too busy to help. He had just been made head ranger and his day was so full of all sorts of pressing tasks there was not much time left over for his son. Or so it seemed to Akimbo.

Akimbo thought about building a tree house. There were plenty of suitable shady trees to choose from, but when he started to look for wood, he found that all the planks which were the right size were earmarked for something else. So he had to abandon the tree house idea.

Then, quite unexpectedly, his father announced over breakfast one morning that

he was going to
have to be away from
home for a few days.

'I'm going over to one of the farms in
the south,' he said. 'There have been reports
of lion attacks on cattle. They want us to
come and deal with the problem.'

Akimbo listened carefully. Lion attacks!
He stared down at the table, wondering
whether his father would let him go with
him. Sometimes he was allowed to go with
the men when they went off into the bush on
a routine trip, but he had never been
permitted to help with anything quite like
this.

He watched his father, waiting for him to
give more details, but the ranger just sipped
at his mug of tea and said nothing more.
Akimbo decided that he should ask him

straight away.

'May I come with you?' he said hesitantly. 'I won't get in the way, I promise you.'

Akimbo's father frowned and shook his head.

'I'm sorry, Akimbo,' he said. 'I'm going to have my hands full and I just won't have time to look after you.'

'But I can look after myself now,' Akimbo protested. 'I won't be any trouble – I promise.'

Akimbo's father looked at his son. He enjoyed having him around when he had small jobs to perform, but an expedition to deal with marauding lions? That was different. And yet, he had to admit that his son was bigger now, and he certainly knew how to keep out of trouble in the bush.

'Well . . .' he began doubtfully. 'You won't

get in the way, will you?'

Akimbo leapt to his feet in delight.

'Of course I won't,' he said. 'And I'm sure I'll be able to help.'

'Mmm,' said his father, still sounding a little unconvinced. 'I don't know about that. But I suppose that there's no harm in your coming with us.'

Akimbo could hardly contain his delight. The boredom which he had been feeling up until now had completely disappeared. He was going off in search of lions – the proudest and most dangerous animal in the bush! He had, of course, seen lions in the distance, and on one occasion they had surprised a sleeping lioness only a very short way away from them, but this sounded as if they were going to get even closer than that!

He wondered if it would be as exciting as

his last adventure.

The tracking down of the ivory poachers and his saving of the elephants had been the most thrilling thing that had happened to him in his life. But it had also been one of the most frightening, and he was pleased it was all over.

They left early the next day, before the sun rose above the hills. The morning air was sharp and fresh, and the men rubbed

their hands together to keep them warm as they waited for the truck to set off. Akimbo sat in the cab with his father, while the men perched in the back with their equipment. His mother had given him a flask of tea and some sandwiches for his breakfast, and as the truck set off along the bumpy road, Akimbo unwrapped his sandwiches and began to eat.

As the sun came up, it painted the plains around them with gold. Flights of birds rose up from the lakes and treetops; herds of zebra stared at the passing vehicle before stampeding off in a cloud of dust; an antelope and its tiny calf skittered in panic across the road in front of them. Akimbo had not slept well that night, as he was too excited by the prospect of the trip. Now, as it became hotter, he found himself dozing off, being woken from time to time by a bump in the road, but drifting back into sleep again.

They stopped once or twice before they reached the farm. The men in the back got out, stretched their legs, and brewed up a pot of tea on a fire of brushwood. Then, at last, just after noon, they saw the farm they were looking for, a cluster of distant buildings surrounded by trees. As the truck drew to a halt outside the farmhouse, the farm dogs barking loudly and defensively, the farmer came out on to the verandah of his house and waved a friendly greeting.

Akimbo sat at the foot of his father's chair while the two men discussed the problem.

'There have been five attacks now,' said the farmer gravely. 'All of them have happened within the last month.'

Akimbo's father nodded. 'Tell me about them,' he said.

The farmer sighed. 'I've lost twelve cattle,' he said. 'In each case it's happened at night. The lion has broken in to the cattle pen and killed one or two beasts. He's dragged them about a bit, trying to get them out, but eventually he's given up and had his meal right there.'

'Has anybody seen it happen?' asked Akimbo's father.

The farmer smiled. 'I put a man on duty at the pen for a few nights, but when he heard the commotion he decided to run back up here. I can't blame him, of course, but it means that he didn't see what happened. He said he thought there was only one lion, though.'

Akimbo's father thought for a while.

'It's probably the same lion,' he said. 'You get one animal that can't be bothered to hunt for prey out in the bush and it picks on a soft target.'

He paused for a few moments before continuing. 'The trouble is that the only way to stop it is to shoot the lion or get it removed. You can't teach them new ways.'

'Do you think you'll be able to trap it?' the farmer asked, sounding rather doubtful.

Akimbo's father laughed. 'It may take us a few days,' he said. 'It may take us a week. But we'll certainly try. And I think that I can say that it'll either catch us or we'll catch it!'

Akimbo swallowed hard. He knew that his father was half-joking, but there would be danger whichever way one looked at it. Still, he had asked to come, and he was definitely not going to change his mind now.

The trap

Later, as they left the farmhouse, Akimbo's father told him of his plan.

'The last thing we want is to shoot the lion,' he explained. 'We'll try to trap him if at all possible.'

'But how do you do that?' asked Akimbo. 'Will you use one of your special darts?'

Akimbo had seen a rhinoceros trapped that way before. The animal had to be moved from one part of the reserve to another and the rangers had shot at it with a special dart gun. The dart had contained a drug which sent the rhino to sleep for half an hour, so the rangers were able to load it into a truck and move it safely.

'We can't use a dart at night,' said his father. 'We won't get close enough to see the lion properly, and if we had lights it would keep well away.'

'So how will we get him?' Akimbo persisted.

'We'll set up a trap,' said his father. 'We'll put a goat in one part of the trap – lions can't resist goat meat – and then when the lion goes in, the door springs shut.'

Akimbo's father made it all sound so simple. But Akimbo thought it could hardly be easy to trap so large a creature as a lion. Would the trap be strong enough? What if the lion lunged against the sides – would they hold?

They walked back together to where the men were standing near the truck. Akimbo's father told them to climb aboard again, and, together with one of the farmer's assistants to show them the way, they set off along the farm track that led to the cattle stockade.

All that afternoon the men worked on the construction of the trap. It was made of stout poles, which they had brought with them, and these were dug into the ground to

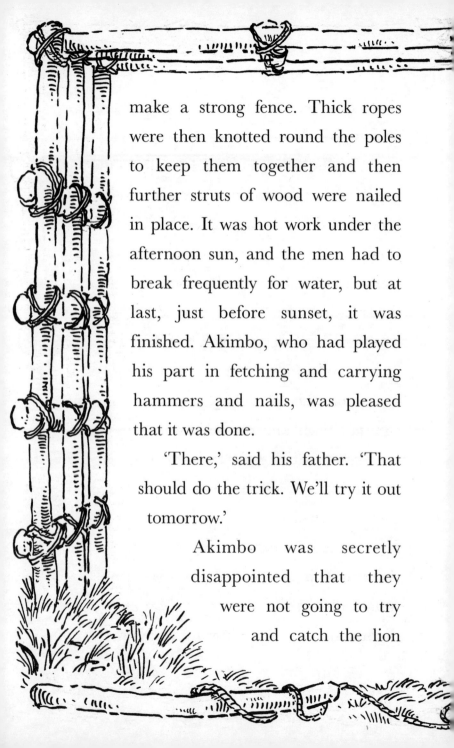

make a strong fence. Thick ropes were then knotted round the poles to keep them together and then further struts of wood were nailed in place. It was hot work under the afternoon sun, and the men had to break frequently for water, but at last, just before sunset, it was finished. Akimbo, who had played his part in fetching and carrying hammers and nails, was pleased that it was done.

'There,' said his father. 'That should do the trick. We'll try it out tomorrow.'

Akimbo was secretly disappointed that they were not going to try and catch the lion

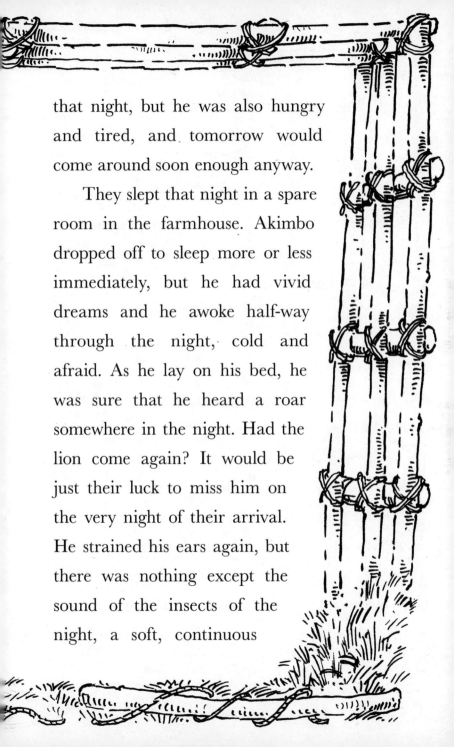

that night, but he was also hungry and tired, and tomorrow would come around soon enough anyway.

They slept that night in a spare room in the farmhouse. Akimbo dropped off to sleep more or less immediately, but he had vivid dreams and he awoke half-way through the night, cold and afraid. As he lay on his bed, he was sure that he heard a roar somewhere in the night. Had the lion come again? It would be just their luck to miss him on the very night of their arrival. He strained his ears again, but there was nothing except the sound of the insects of the night, a soft, continuous clicking and screeching that he knew would last until the first light of morning.

They took the farmer out the next day to show him the trap. No lions had come last night, in spite of what Akimbo thought he had heard, and the cattle were all counted and found to be safe.

'It's almost five days since he attacked,' said the farmer. 'I'm sure that he'll be back soon.'

'We'll be ready,' said Akimbo's father. 'We'll stake out the bait tonight and see what happens.'

Akimbo tried hard to conceal his mounting excitement. It was a long time until nightfall, and he wished that it would come sooner. But he was not worried by the slowness of the hours, only whether his father might tell him to stay in the farmhouse tonight. If that happened, he would miss all the excitement, and he could not bear the thought of that.

'Where are we going to hide tonight?' he asked his father cautiously, once the farmer had gone.

Akimbo's father looked down at his son.

'Oh, I don't think you should be out here,' he said. 'It'll be far too dangerous. You must stay in the farmhouse, as you did last night.'

Akimbo's face fell. It was just what he had feared. What was the point of coming all this way if he was going to miss the real excitement? He looked at his father, and his disappointment must have been written so large all over his face that his father suddenly seemed to soften.

'Do you really want to spend the night

out here with us?' he asked. 'It'll be cold and uncomfortable. You won't have a nice warm bed to sleep in.'

'I do want to do it,' Akimbo pleaded. 'I don't want to miss what happens.'

Akimbo's father seemed to waver for a moment before he gave in.

'All right,' he said. 'As long as you keep well away from everything.'

Akimbo was happy to agree. He was keen to see what happened when the lion came, but not at all eager to get too close.

There was little to do that afternoon, and so Akimbo spent his time wandering about the farmyard. He helped one of the stockmen round up some sheep, and he was given a roasted maize cob as a reward. After that, though, it was just a question of waiting.

At about four o'clock, Akimbo's father hailed him from the truck.

'We're going now,' he called out. 'Come along.'

Akimbo raced over to join his father and the men. He noticed that one of the men was holding a young goat, and Akimbo realised that this must be the bait. He felt sorry for the little creature, with its frightened black eyes and its sad, hopeless bleating, but he knew that if the trap worked it would be safe from the lion. But would the trap work? His father seemed so confident that it would, but Akimbo himself was not so sure.

Akimbo shivered as he thought of it. Perhaps it would have been better to stay in the farmhouse after all.

But it was far too late to think these thoughts, as the journey had begun, and whether Akimbo liked it or not there was no turning back.

Lion!

The cattle were already in their stockade when the truck drew up. The men jumped out of the back as they came to a halt and immediately set about the task of preparing the trap. The goat, still bleating sadly, was taken into a special compartment at the top of the cage, and bundled in. It stood unsteadily on its feet and looked about it, wondering what was happening.

It's just as well you don't know, thought Akimbo sadly.

Then Akimbo's father checked the mechanism. It was quite simple really. The idea was that when the lion came into the cattle stockade it would smell or hear the goat. It would be drawn to it and would soon find its route into the maze of poles. Once in, though, it would trip a piece of twine which ran through two pegs in the ground, and this would bring down a roughly-made door behind it. The goat, which was enclosed within a small pen at the top, would get a terrible fright, but should be out of reach of the lion's claws.

Of course the lion could be expected to be angry, and would soon realise that it was trapped. At that stage, Akimbo's father could safely go up to it and fire one of his drugged darts. He could leave that until the morning, though, when they would bring the travelling cage they had with them and could manhandle the lion into that.

'Right,' said Akimbo's father once he had finished his check. 'Everything seems to be in order. Now we must all get out of here.'

'Are we going to stay in the truck?' asked Akimbo, thinking that that would be the warmest place to be.

The ranger shook his head.

'No,' he said. 'That's going back to the farm. There's no need for all the men to stay out here tonight, and it would also increase the risk of the lion smelling human beings. If he did that, he'd keep well away.'

'So it's just us who are going to stay?' asked Akimbo.

'Yes,' said his father. 'But you've still got a chance to go back, if you want to.'

Akimbo struggled with himself. It was

one thing to talk about staying out all night in the middle of the bush, with lions about; it was another thing to be actually about to do it. But he was determined now. He would not change his mind.

'No thank you,' he replied. 'This is where I want to be.'

'All right,' said his father, signalling to the men. 'On your way now.'

They watched the truck bouncing away in the distance over the rutted farm track. Soon it was only a cloud of dust, and then that too disappeared, and they were alone.

'There's a clump of trees over there,' said Akimbo's father, pointing to a place a little way away from the stockade. 'We can go in there. That should give us a good bit of cover.'

They made their way over to the trees

and found a place where they could sit and where they would be reasonably well concealed from view. Akimbo's father picked up a stick, took out his penknife, and began to whittle away at the wood. As he did so, he whistled a song which Akimbo had always enjoyed when he was younger, and which made him smile now.

'You like that tune, don't you?' said his father. 'Did I ever tell you the words?'

Akimbo shook his head.

'Well, it's about a lion hunt,' explained his father. 'It's an old, old song about the days when our fathers and grandfathers hunted lions.'

Akimbo laughed.

'Would you sing it now?' he asked. 'I'm sure it will make me feel braver.'

Akimbo's father smiled at the thought, and, as the sun went burning down, a great, friendly red ball, he sang the old song to his son. Soon it was dark, and above them a thousand thousand stars appeared in the African night.

'Sleep if you wish,' said Akimbo's father quietly. 'I shall keep watch. Don't worry.'

Akimbo was not sure how long he had been asleep. He awoke, feeling sore from lying on the hard ground, and he rubbed vigorously at his legs to make them feel better.

'Has anything happened?' he whispered to his father, who was sitting beside him, his rifle laid across his lap.

'No,' said his father, his voice low.

'Nothing yet. You can go back to sleep if you like.'

Akimbo lay down again, but he was far from sleep.

'I could try counting the stars,' he said to himself, looking at the silver fields above him. 'But I'd run out of numbers.'

He thought of the goat, and wondered whether it would be sleeping. Would it be frightened, being out here in this strange place, far from all the other goats? Or would it accept the change naturally, as animals so often seemed to do?

It was then that he heard it, and the sound made him sit bolt upright. The goat was bleating – a clear, sharp sound rising above the insect sounds of the night.

Akimbo turned to his father, who had also heard the sound and who had laid a

hand on his son's arm.

'It's sensed something,' his father whispered. 'We must be very quiet now.'

Akimbo peered in the direction of the trap, but it was only a dim shape in the darkness. In the stockade, one or two of the cattle moved, and then there was a bleating again. It was louder now, with a note of panic.

Suddenly there was more movement. The cattle moved from one side of the stockade to the other, and bellowed in fright. Akimbo strained his eyes against the darkness. He looked up at the sky: the moon was behind a cloud, and it was difficult to see, but then, slowly, the cloud passed by and

the moonlight flooded back.

There was a thud, and then, loud and unmistakeable, a roar. A lion was in the cage, and had struck out at the wooden bars that separated it from the terrified goat. Akimbo's father rose to his feet.

'He's in the trap,' he said. 'That's it.'

'What are you going to do?' asked Akimbo urgently.

'I'm going to take a look,' his father replied. 'You stay right here, understand?'

There was a tone in his father's voice that made Akimbo realise that it was no use trying to argue. He crouched where he was as his father crept forwards towards the trap. The noise had died down now, and Akimbo wondered what the lion was doing. Surely it would not have accepted its captivity so quickly? Yet he was sure now he could see it in the trap – a large, dark shape, half-lying, half-standing.

In his desire to see more clearly, Akimbo rose to his knees and peered forwards. As he did so, his leg brushed against something cold and hard. It was his father's rifle.

'Your gun!' he called out. 'Father! Your gun!'

Akimbo's father looked back. He had not meant to leave the rifle behind and it would be dangerous to inspect the trap unarmed. He turned round, and, as he did so, the lion, who had been watching him cautiously, moved. Unknown to both Akimbo and his father, the trap had not worked. The lion had found its way in, but the mechanism which should have brought the gate down behind it had failed. Then, when the lion saw the man coming towards it through the moonlight, it had lain low, watching to see what would happen.

It was Akimbo who saw the lion stalk out of the trap. He called out to his father again, and the ranger spun round. He was now face to face with a crouching, angry lion, separated only by twenty or thirty paces. There was no knowing what the lion would do, but Akimbo's father realised that whatever happened, he was in the greatest possible danger.

Left behind

Akimbo thought quickly. If his father ran for safety now, that could prompt the lion to attack. If he himself ran towards his father, that could have the same effect. The rifle: that was the only thing that stood between them and disaster. He bent down and picked it up.

Akimbo had watched his father practising with his rifle, but had never used it himself. He knew about the safety catch, though, and he slipped it off and drew back the weapon's bolt. The sound was loud in the night, and he wondered whether the lion had heard it.

Akimbo drew the rifle up to his shoulder and looked down the barrel. For a moment or two he lost sight of the lion, but then he saw it again. It was moving again, down on its haunches, as if circling its prey. He steadied the weapon, and tried to line up the sights, but it was difficult in the darkness.

Then he had the lion in the sights and his finger moved to the trigger. But he stopped. If he fired, could he be sure that he would not just wound the lion, which would then become enraged and take his father within a few bounds?

'Fire!' he heard his father shout. 'Fire in the air!'

Akimbo moved the barrel up sharply and

squeezed the trigger. There was a shattering explosion that made his ears ring with sharp fury. He drew back the bolt and pulled the trigger again, reeling from the kick of the rifle's recoil. Then he lowered the rifle and looked towards the lion. It had disappeared.

Akimbo's father came running towards him.

'Well done!' he cried, gently taking the rifle from his son's hands. 'That sent her off in a hurry.'

'Her?' said Akimbo, still a little dazed. 'Was it a lioness?'

'Yes,' said his father. 'It was. Your first shot sent her scurrying off into the bush, and I should imagine that the second just drove the message further home.'

Akimbo sat down. He was still feeling shaky, and the ringing in his ears seemed louder than ever.

'We'll go over in a moment and see why the trap didn't spring,' said Akimbo's father. 'And I won't leave my rifle here this time.'

'Will we have to try to catch her again tomorrow night?' asked Akimbo.

'I doubt it,' said his father. 'I should think that she's learned her lesson for the time being. Lions don't like to stay around places where they've heard gunfire.'

They walked over to the trap. The goat was still bleating, from shock, they thought, but when they arrived at the trap they saw that it was for a very different reason. The trap had now sprung, and the gate was down, and there was a lion inside. But it was a very small lion indeed.

'A cub!' exclaimed Akimbo. 'Look! We've caught her cub.'

* * *

The next morning, when the men brought the truck back, Akimbo's father explained to them all what had happened during the night.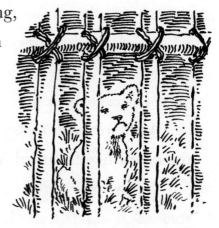

'When the lioness came out of the trap,' he said, 'she must have tripped the mechanism. But her cub was still inside and couldn't get out. That's why she didn't charge me. Then, when Akimbo fired the rifle, she panicked and ran away.'

'What are we going to do with the little one?' asked one of the men. 'Can we let him go?'

Akimbo's father scratched his head.

'I just don't know,' he said. 'I suspect

that the mother won't be coming back now, so we can't really leave him. He'll die of starvation.'

Akimbo looked out into the night. 'Won't she wait for him?' he asked. 'Don't you think she'll return for him once we've gone away?'

'No,' said Akimbo's father. 'I've seen this sort of thing before. I imagine that she's been shot at by somebody some time ago, probably even wounded – that's why she's taken to going for easy prey like cattle. She'll be really frightened now.'

Akimbo tugged at his father's elbow.

'We could take him back with us,' he urged. 'We could feed him at the house.'

The ranger sighed.

'Who's going to do that?' he asked. 'I'm far too busy these days to be spending my time feeding lion cubs.'

'I'll do it,' offered Akimbo. 'I've got the time.'

'And when he grows up?' asked Akimbo's father. 'What happens then?'

'That's a long time off,' said Akimbo. 'But he could go and live in the reserve.'

Akimbo's father thought for a few moments. He glanced down at the lion cub, nestling softly in his son's arms. The little creature looked so gentle and trusting that it was impossible to resist him.

'All right,' he said. 'I suppose so.'

Akimbo's mother was astonished when they arrived home later that day with Akimbo clutching a wriggling bundle of mewing fur.

'A lion!' she exclaimed. 'Surely that's not the lion who's been causing all the trouble.'

Akimbo's father laughed.

'No,' he said. 'But I'm afraid it was his mother.'

'We caught him by mistake,' explained Akimbo. 'His mother left him behind in the trap.'

'I see,' said Akimbo's mother, bending down to inspect the little animal as Akimbo placed him gently on the floor. Then she looked up, puzzled.

'Why would any lioness leave a little cub like this?' she asked. 'What happened?'

Akimbo explained, and while he did so, the cub nuzzled warmly at his ankles.

Then the little lion stood unsteadily on its feet. It looked up at Akimbo's mother, blinked, and then sat down.

'He's weak,' she said. 'Look, his legs are unsteady.'

'He'll have to be fed soon,' Akimbo's father said. 'You should get some milk and warm it up for him.'

Akimbo poured a little bit of milk into a saucepan and then put it on to the stove to heat up. It took a few minutes, but soon the milk was warm to the touch. Then he poured it into a large saucer and placed it before the cub.

The tiny lion looked down at the plate, sniffed uncertainly, and then turned his head away.

'We're going to have trouble feeding him,' said Akimbo's father gravely. 'These creatures are hard to raise in captivity. I'm afraid he might not make it.'

Akimbo shook his head. 'He'll eat,' he said. 'I'm sure he will.'

He pushed the saucer towards the cub again and then pushed his nose down into the milk. The cub snuffled and drew his head away sharply, giving Akimbo a reproachful look as he did so.

'It's strange to him,' said Akimbo's father. 'He's used to lioness milk, I'm afraid.'

Akimbo's mother, who had gone out of the room, now returned.

'Let's try this,' she said, showing her son a baby's bottle. 'You certainly liked it when you were a baby.'

They poured the milk into the bottle and then pushed the teat into the little lion's mouth. He spat out the teat straight away and tried to walk away from them on his unsteady legs.

Akimbo was disappointed. He could see that the cub was weak, and it saddened him to think of how hungry it must be. If only it would realise that the milk was good for it.

'We'll try again later,' said Akimbo's mother. 'In the meantime, let's put him in the old chicken run. He should be safe there.'

They carried the cub out of the kitchen and placed him gently in the wire run which Akimbo's mother used to use for her hens. It was a good place for the little animal, as it was shady and he would be able to move about without being able to escape. He stood up, looked about his new surroundings, and then lay down again.

'We'll try to feed him again in half an hour,' said Akimbo's mother. 'He should be used to his new home by then. By the way, what are you going to call him?'

'Simba,' said Akimbo simply. 'Because that means lion.'

'Simba,' repeated Akimbo's mother, nodding her approval. 'That sounds like a very good name for him.'

Becoming friends

That night, just before he went to bed, Akimbo took a dish of milk out to Simba's run and put it in front of him. The tiny lion sniffed at the milk, just as he had done before, and then turned away.

'You must eat,' Akimbo urged. 'It's no good just turning up your nose like that.'

Simba looked at Akimbo in a puzzled sort of way. He was not at all sure about his surroundings, and he was uncertain whether or not to trust this boy who kept putting a dish of strange-smelling liquid in front of him.

Akimbo picked up the dish of milk and moved it to a corner of the run.

'I'll leave it there,' he said gently. 'When you get really hungry in the night, that's the time you should have it.'

And with that he turned away, leaving the little lion by itself in the run. It made him sad to leave Simba, as he imagined that the little creature would be missing his mother. But he would get used to that – animals always did – and he would have plenty of friends in the game camp – Akimbo would see to that.

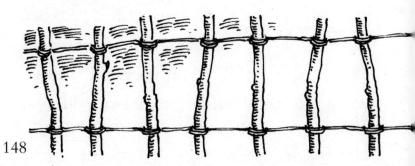

The next morning, the first thing that Akimbo did when he awoke was to leap out of bed and make his way as fast as he could to Simba's run. The lion was standing near the gate, his paws up on the wooden struts, and when he saw Akimbo he let out a soft mew of greeting.

Akimbo ruffled his fur, which seemed to give him pleasure, and then he looked over at the corner of the run where he had left the dish of milk. It had clearly not been touched.

'Listen,' he said, as he picked up the small bundle of yellow fur and stroked his back. 'If you don't eat, you'll just get weaker

and weaker. You must try.'

But Simba was not interested in the milk, and try as he might Akimbo could not get him to change his mind.

'So he's not eating,' said Akimbo's father when his son spoke to him at breakfast time. 'That doesn't look good, I'm afraid.'

Akimbo's heart sank. He would give anything to get the lion cub to eat, but if he wouldn't take milk, then what hope was there?

'What will happen?' he asked his father. 'Surely he'll get so hungry that he'll drink the milk, even if he doesn't like it.'

Akimbo's father shook his head. 'I'm afraid not,' he said. 'Animals can be strange that way. Sometimes they just won't eat in captivity, and there's nothing you can do about it.'

Akimbo hung his head. 'I don't want Simba to starve,' he said sadly. 'I don't want him to die.'

For a few moments his father said nothing, then he leaned forwards and patted his son's shoulder.

'There is somebody who might be able to help,' he said. 'One of the other rangers raised a lion cub once. I can ask him how he did it. He may have some ideas. Would you like that?'

Akimbo was overjoyed. He was sure that there was some way of getting Simba to eat – all he had to do was to hear about it.

That afternoon, the ranger called at the house and asked Akimbo to show him where Simba was kept. Akimbo took him out to the run, where they saw Simba lying, panting in the heat. The little lion was now quite weak, and didn't even bother to rise to his feet when the humans came into his run.

The ranger sighed. 'He's not in good shape,' he said. 'Has he eaten anything at all?'

'No,' said Akimbo. 'Nothing.'

The ranger walked over to Simba and gently opened the cub's jaws. He peered into his mouth, and then felt around his stomach.

'I can't see anything wrong,' he said at last. 'What have you been giving him?'

'Milk,' said Akimbo. 'I showed him some meat, but he wasn't interested.'

The ranger laughed. 'He wouldn't be,' he said. 'Just yet. Tell me – has your mother got any honey?'

'Yes,' said Akimbo. 'I have it on my bread every day.'

'And do you like it?' asked the ranger, smiling.

'Of course,' replied Akimbo. 'I think it's delicious.'

'Well,' said the ranger, 'so do lion cubs. Now you go and mix up two or three spoons of honey in some warm milk and then bring it out here. You may be surprised by what you see.'

Akimbo ran back to the kitchen and mixed the milk and honey as he had been instructed. Then he dashed  back to the run, trying not to spill any of the precious sweet liquid on his way. Handing the dish to the ranger, he stood back and watched while it was placed right under Simba's nose.

For a short time the lion did nothing. Then, slowly, his nose began to twitch.

'Come on,' urged the ranger. 'Time for lunch.'

Simba had now staggered uncertainly to his feet, his nose still sniffing at the edge of the dish. Then, as if it was the most natural thing in the world for him to do, his tongue shot out and began to lick up the rich white liquid, slopping it everywhere about him as he did so.

'There,' said the ranger. 'That's the end of his feeding problems, Akimbo!'

Over the next few days, Simba drank more milk than Akimbo would have thought possible. Fortunately, there was no shortage of supplies, as the rangers kept several cows for their own use, but it was not long before

Akimbo's mother was sending off for more honey.

'This lion of yours is going to eat us out of house and home,' she laughed. 'Look at how fat he's becoming!'

Akimbo's mother was right. The skin about Simba's stomach was now stretched tight, and when he walked it was with more of a waddle than the swagger one might expect of a lion. It was difficult not to laugh at him, and it was certainly hard to remember that in due course he would grow up into the most fearsome of beasts. It seemed impossible to imagine that this funny, rolling bundle of lion fur could ever be like the lions Akimbo had seen snarling and growling over their prey.

When he was quite sure that Simba was used to his new surroundings, Akimbo allowed him out of the run. At first the little lion seemed unwilling to leave the security of his cage, but after a short while his natural curiosity got the better of him and he took his first few hesitant steps outside. He was happy to follow Akimbo, and was soon trotting contentedly behind him as he made his way from the run to the house. Every so often he would stop, sit down, and scratch himself, but then he would bound up again, tripping over Akimbo's feet, jumping up at him playfully.

Akimbo felt tremendously proud. It was marvellous to have a lion – a lion all of his own. And he knew, too, that Simba realised that he belonged to him. Each morning, when he went out to the run, there would be Simba, waiting impatiently for his master. As Akimbo opened the gate, the tiny lion would be all over him, licking and purring, just like a great cat. Then they would play games together, and perhaps go for a walk. As Akimbo walked along, Simba gambolling beside him, he felt that he was probably the very luckiest boy in all Africa.

Lion at school

Three weeks after Simba's arrival, it was time for Akimbo to go back to school. It was hard having to say goodbye to Simba each morning. The little lion whimpered as he saw Akimbo leave, and for a long time afterwards he lay on the earthen floor of his run and pined. Akimbo spent his time thinking about Simba, so he found it difficult to concentrate on his work.

'What are you thinking of?' his teacher demanded. 'You seem to be in a constant daydream these days!'

When Akimbo came back at the end of each day, Simba would leap about him with delight, just as a dog welcomes back his master.

'That little lion has been missing you,' said Akimbo's mother. 'I tried to play with him but he would have nothing of it.'

Akimbo was secretly pleased by this. It made him happy to think that he was the most important person in Simba's life. He decided to teach Simba tricks, and he trained him to pad along beside him when he went for walks. At first he had been worried that Simba might try to escape, but soon he realised that the lion only wanted to be with him and that he had no thought of leaving.

Everybody was very amused by the sight of Akimbo with his lion and soon the story of the friendship between lion and boy had reached towns and cities far away. A reporter came to write an article about Akimbo, and a photographer spent a whole day taking photographs of the two together.

Simba was growing bigger now. He was no longer the tiny, helpless little cub which they had found in the trap; he was now much larger, and much stronger too. His appetite had increased, of course, and he had long since moved on from the dishes of milk and honey. Now he ate meat, enthusiastically tearing at bones and gnawing at them until every scrap of food had been taken off.

Although he had grown, Simba was still gentle. When he played with Akimbo – when they tumbled down on the ground together and pretended to be wrestling with one another – never once did he allow his claws to scratch the boy. And although he might try to grab Akimbo's leg in a playful way, his teeth, now quite large and sharp, would never cause the slightest damage.

Yet Akimbo knew that sooner or later the cub would become a young lion, and that was the point at which people would begin to ask questions. Simba's run was far too small for a fully-grown lion, and was far too weak to contain him. Would anybody feel safe when Simba roamed the village and began to roar?

A few months after Simba's arrival, Akimbo had gone to school one day rather later than usual, and had been scolded by the teacher, who believed in strict punctuality. The day got off to a bad start.

It was shortly after the children had

had their break that it happened. Akimbo was sitting on his bench when he heard the shouting outside.

'A lion!' somebody yelled. 'There's a lion coming!'

The whole class rose to its feet and looked out of the window. There, coming along the path towards the school, trotting along with his head held high in the air, was Simba. For a moment or two, Akimbo did not recognise him – this lion looked much bigger than Simba, but when he saw the patch of dark fur under his chin he knew immediately who it was.

The teacher did not know what to do. He raised his hand and then he dropped it. Meanwhile, Simba had reached the edge of the clearing in which the school stood and was looking about him, sniffing at the air inquisitively.

Everything might have been all right had the teacher's cook not come round the corner of the school building at the wrong time. She had not seen Simba, and walked unsuspectingly into the middle of the school yard.

Then she stopped. For a moment or two, the two of them stood absolutely still. The woman seemed to have frozen to the spot, and as for Simba, he wondered why she had stopped walking. Did she want to play? Did she want him to chase her?

As if suddenly pricked by a great pin, the woman screamed at the top of her voice and gave a leap backwards. For Simba this was a

signal. So she did want to play after all! Bounding forwards, he chased her, soon caught up with her and leapt playfully on to her back.

Inside the classroom the teacher shouted and began to dash for the door.

'No!' called out Akimbo. 'Let me go.'

The teacher tried to stop him, but Akimbo pushed past and was soon out in the yard. Simba was now standing on top of the woman, who was lying on the ground, moaning and sobbing with fright.

'Simba!' called Akimbo. 'Here! Here!'

When Simba saw and heard his master, he was overjoyed. Leaving the poor woman where she was, he bounded across to Akimbo and began to lick joyfully at his knees and ankles. Akimbo bent down and ruffled the fur around the lion's neck.

'You're not to come here,' he whispered. 'You'll get us both into trouble.'

Akimbo was right. There was trouble, and an awful lot of it. The poor woman was unhurt but she was, of course, very angry, as was the teacher. Still keeping a good distance away from Simba, the teacher ordered Akimbo to take the lion back home and to wait there. He would come across later that day to speak to Akimbo's father.

Akimbo walked back, sunk in

unhappiness. Simba seemed perfectly cheerful, but then he didn't know what trouble he had caused.

'I hope they don't try to take you away from me,' Akimbo said as they made their way home. 'I couldn't bear to lose you, Simba, I really couldn't!'

Back to the wilds

The teacher arrived later that afternoon and went straight to Akimbo's father. From a distance Akimbo watched the two men as they stood outside the game reserve office and talked. The teacher gestured from time to time, moving his hands sharply as if to underline a point, and Akimbo could tell that he was very angry. Eventually they stopped talking. Akimbo's father shook hands with the teacher and went back to his office. The teacher got back on his bicycle and cycled away, glancing uncomfortably over in the direction of Akimbo's house, just in case a lion should come bounding out towards him.

When his father came home at five o'clock, Akimbo had prepared himself for the worst.

'I have to talk to you,' the ranger said. 'I think you'll know what it's about.'

Akimbo nodded glumly. 'I'm sorry,' he said. 'I didn't mean it to happen.'

'I know that,' said his father. 'I'm not really blaming you for what happened. But I'm afraid it does mean that . . .'

He paused for a moment, watching his son. Akimbo was looking at him, struggling against the tears, but unable to hold them back.

'It means that Simba will have to go,' said the ranger. 'We can't have a grown lion around here. It's just too dangerous.'

'But he's always so gentle,' protested Akimbo. 'He wouldn't harm anybody.'

'That may be so,' said his father. 'But we can't take a risk. You can't change a lion's nature for good. Sooner or later he might attack somebody. It's in him – right deep down inside – you just can't make him into anything but what he is – a lion.'

Akimbo was silent. He knew that what his father said was probably true and that he would have to say goodbye to Simba.

'So,' said the ranger finally. 'We'll take him out tomorrow and try to reintroduce him to the wild. It would be better than sending him off to some zoo.'

It was bitter news for Akimbo, but he knew that it would be much better for Simba to live his life with other lions in the

wild, rather than in the cramped and uncomfortable quarters which he might be given in some distant zoo. That evening, after he had fed Simba, he spent some time just sitting with the sleepy lion, letting the animal nuzzle at him fondly.

'I'm going to miss you so much,' he said. 'Will you miss me too?'

Simba pushed his face against him and gave him a lick. It was his way of answering, thought Akimbo, and he was sure that it meant yes.

The next morning they set off early. Akimbo sat with Simba in the back of the truck, while his father drove out deep into the reserve. There was a place he knew – a place by a river – where there were several prides of lions, and this would be a place where Simba would have as good a chance as anywhere. You couldn't just throw a small lion out into the bush and expect it to survive – Simba had never been taught how to hunt. But with any luck he would be found by other lions, and some of the females might take pity on him. There might be one who had lost her cub and who was looking for another; it had been known to happen that way before.

It was a long journey, but at last they arrived. Akimbo's father stopped the truck under a tree that grew by the edge of the river and the three of them got out. Simba was excited by his new surroundings, and dashed round inquisitively. He went down to the water's edge and after looking at it suspiciously for a few moments, dipped his nose in and drank.

Akimbo and his father watched as Simba looked about him. He sniffed at the ground, seeming to find something that interested him, and he even gave a low growl. Then he came back, and tugged at Akimbo's shirt, as if wanting him to go off for a walk with him.

'He likes it here,' said Akimbo's father. 'I think he might be all right now.'

It was hard to leave. As Akimbo slammed the door of the truck shut behind him, Simba, who had been walking in some tall grass nearby, cocked his head and looked back at them, as if to say: 'Surely you can't be going without me. Just hold on, I have a little more exploring to do.'

But they did not wait. Akimbo's father switched on the engine, engaged the gears, and with a rapid turn began to drive away. Akimbo looked back, and for a moment he saw Simba leaping out of the tall grass and looking towards them in a puzzled way. Then he was obscured by the dust from the wheels of the truck and he could see him no

more. His friend was alone, and for the rest of the journey back Akimbo felt his heart cold and sad within him.

It was difficult to get used to the empty run at the back of the house, and for a while Akimbo preferred not to go out that way. It was painful to think of Simba all alone in the vastness of the bush. Had he been found by other lions? Had he gone hungry? Had he been cold that night, with nowhere to snuggle for warmth? Akimbo hoped that Simba was all right, but he knew how hard life was in the wild. It would not have been easy for the young lion – he was sure of that.

Several months later, Akimbo's father said that he could come with him on one of his trips deep into the bush. Akimbo was delighted. They would be away for at least two days, and he always loved camping out under the stars.

On the first night they were out, they found themselves not far from the river where Simba had been released. They set up camp that night, below the very tree where they had stopped on the sad day on which they had said farewell. Akimbo's father seemed to have forgotten that this was the place, but Akimbo remembered every detail. He still thought and worried about Simba all the time. Perhaps

there was a chance, just the slightest of chances, that they would see Simba again.

In the morning, Akimbo awoke earlier than his father, and he crawled out of the tent to get himself a mug of water from the water bottle in the truck. As he did so, he suddenly realised that he was not alone, that there was something on the other side of the river.

He stood quite still, not wanting to give away his presence. The grass and bushes on that side, which were thick and luxuriant, had parted, and five or six lions had come down to the water's edge to drink. It was a beautiful sight to witness, especially since the lions had not seen him and were quite at ease.

Akimbo watched as a lioness dipped her head to the surface of the water and then raised it up again as the water ran down her throat. He watched as the leader of the pride, a large male with a mane of near-black, moved forwards to quench his thirst.

Then he saw him. There was a lion, a young lion, just behind the female, and he came forwards now and looked at the water. Akimbo knew who it was. He was as certain of it as he could be of anything. He knew in his bones that this was Simba.

For a moment he did nothing, but then, unable to contain himself any longer, he moved forwards and called out as he did so.

'Simba!' His voice carried easily across the water, and the lions gave a start.

The male lion roared, and then spun round and darted off into the bush, quickly followed by the others. All except Simba – he stayed, looking across the water at the boy on the other side.

Akimbo moved forwards a further step, bringing himself into the shallows. It was not a broad river, and now only a short stretch of water separated the lion and the boy.

The movement disturbed Simba. For a moment he hesitated, but then his natural instincts got the better of him.

'Come back!' cried Akimbo, but it was too late. The river remained between them, and it always would, in a way. Akimbo knew that there was no going back. Simba was where he should be – with other lions – and Akimbo understood that this had to be.

Akimbo turned away from the river and made his way back to the tent. He was relieved that Simba was safe, and although he was sad to have seen him only for so short a time, the fact that his friend had remembered him made him feel happy – and proud.

He looked back over his shoulder, at the river and at the bush beyond.

'Goodbye, Simba!' he called out softly. 'And good luck!'

AKIMBO
AND THE
CROCODILE
MAN

This book is for Philip
and Mary Magee

Contents

An unusual visitor   189

A dangerous search begins   203

Catching a crocodile!   215

The baby crocodiles arrive   227

Crocodile attack   235

A dangerous swim   249

Getting help   259

An unusual visitor

Akimbo was sitting in his favourite cool place on the verandah, looking down the long, dusty track that led to the house. It was the middle of a hot African afternoon and the bush was alive with the screech of insects. Overhead, the empty blue sky seemed to go on for ever and ever. Nothing stirred.

Suddenly Akimbo saw a cloud of dust in the distance. He stood up, straining his eyes to get a better view. Yes, he thought.

This is it.

'Look!' he shouted to his mother who was somewhere inside the house. 'Look! Our visitor is coming.'

Akimbo's mother joined him on the verandah. The dust cloud was bigger now and they could see what was throwing it up as it bumped its way over the track. It was a large white truck.

'Go off and tell your father,' she said. 'He will want to know that his guest has arrived safely.'

Akimbo ran down the path that

led to the ranger station. He made his way to the half-open door, with its 'Chief Ranger' sign, and peered in.

'Our visitor is here,' he said from the doorway.

Akimbo's father looked up from his desk and smiled. He was clearly pleased to hear the news.

'Good,' he said. 'So the crocodile man has arrived at last!'

When they got back to the house, the white truck had already drawn up at the front door. Akimbo and his father climbed the steps to the verandah, where they found the visitor sitting in one of the canvas chairs, sipping a cup of tea which Akimbo's mother had prepared for him after his long journey.

Akimbo's father shook hands with the man, who then turned to Akimbo and gave him a friendly smile.

'So you're Akimbo,' he said. 'I've heard a lot about you.'

Akimbo reached out shyly and shook the visitor's hand.

'My name's John,' said the man.

Akimbo looked up at him. John was very tall, he noticed, and had a warm, friendly face. But there was something else which he noticed – all the way down his right arm there ran a long, thick scar, punctured here and there by ridges where weals had healed up. Akimbo tried not to stare, but it was hard to avoid doing so, and John noticed the boy's gaze on his arm.

'Yes,' he said jokingly. 'That was quite a bite.'

Akimbo looked away, embarrassed, but it was obvious that John did not mind.

'A crocodile,' he said. 'Not a big one actually. It was only a couple of years old but it took me by surprise and it managed to make quite a mess before I dealt with it.'

Akimbo's father gave a shudder.

'I've always kept well away from those creatures,' he said. 'I don't know what you see in them.'

John laughed. 'But they're fascinating,' he said. 'They're the most interesting animals in Africa.'

Akimbo's father was not convinced.

'Give me lions any time,' he said. 'Or leopards. Or any of the others we have. But crocodiles – no thank you!'

Akimbo did not see their guest until supper-time that night. His father took John across to the ranger station and the two of them did not return until shortly before seven. As they sat down at the table and began their meal, Akimbo made every effort to keep his eyes off John's injured arm, but once again he found it hard to do so. How had the crocodile got him? he wondered. Had John been in the water, or out of it when it happened? And had he saved himself, or had there been somebody there to help him?

As the meal progressed, John turned to Akimbo and began to tell him about himself.

'I'm a zoologist,' he said. 'I spend all my time studying animals and writing up my findings for people to read.'

Akimbo was fascinated. 'Have you written a book?' he asked.

John nodded.

'Yes,' he said. 'I've written a book all about crocodiles.'

'I've seen it,' chipped in Akimbo's father. 'They have it in town.'

Akimbo was most impressed. He had never met anybody who had written a book before – especially a book about crocodiles. He wondered if he would be able to find it at his school. He doubted it somehow, as there were not many books in the school library and those that were there seemed to be about science and mathematics and subjects like that. If only they had books about crocodiles!

'And what are you going to be doing here?' asked Akimbo's mother. Like her

husband, she did not like crocodiles either.

The crocodile man sat back in his chair.

'I'm going to be starting a project on egg hatching,' he said. 'I want to try to find out how many of the newly-hatched crocodiles survive the first year of life.'

Akimbo was surprised to hear about the hatching. He did not even know that crocodiles laid eggs. It seemed so strange to think of a great creature like that coming from something as small as an egg. He wondered if you could eat a crocodile's egg, and whether it would taste at all like a hen's egg. He did not want to try this, but perhaps he would find out about it if he managed to get hold of a book on crocodiles.

John went on to explain what he planned to do. He wanted to try to catch a female crocodile and all her baby crocodiles and to put tags on them. Then, a year later, he would return to the same spot and see how many of the tagged crocodiles could still be found in the area.

This all sounded really interesting to Akimbo. But how did one tag a crocodile? He could not imagine that it would be easy.

'Won't it be dangerous?' he asked. 'I wouldn't like to try to catch the mother crocodile.'

John chuckled. 'Yes,' he replied. 'It can be dangerous. In fact, that's how this happened.'

He pointed to his torn right

arm, answering the question which Akimbo had been longing to ask.

'We'll net them,' John went on, turning to Akimbo's father. 'I'll need three or four of your men,' he said. 'And perhaps you'd like to help as well?'

Akimbo's father raised his hands in horror.

'No, thank you,' he said, quickly adding: 'But I'm sure that some of my men won't mind helping you.'

Akimbo saw his chance.

'Nor would I,' he blurted out. 'I wouldn't mind coming.'

There was a silence at the table. The crocodile man turned and looked at Akimbo.

'Are you sure?' he said. 'I'd be very happy for you to come and watch.'

'I'd love to,' said Akimbo as quickly as

he could, casting a doubtful glance in his father's direction.

Akimbo's father sighed. They had had this argument before, when Akimbo had insisted on going with him to catch a rogue lion which had been raiding cattle pens at the edge of the game park. That adventure had ended with the bringing back of a motherless lion cub. Would this one end with a pet crocodile wandering about the place?

'Please,' Akimbo begged. 'Please say it's all right.'

Akimbo's father looked at the crocodile man, then back at his son.

'Very well,' he said. 'But remember, I don't want you bringing back any little crocodiles.'

'I promise I won't,' insisted Akimbo.

'And I don't want any part of you bitten off!'

added Akimbo's mother sternly. 'Not even a little finger!'

'I promise that won't happen either,' said John, his eyes sparkling.

And with that it was settled. Akimbo would be a member of the crocodile man's team.

A dangerous search begins

They set off the next morning, just the two of them, Akimbo and his new friend John. It was a bright, warm morning, and as they travelled over the rough bush track they disturbed a number of animals who were out finding food before the real heat of the day. They saw baboons, and several families of warthogs, and, as they turned a corner, a rhinoceros lumbered off into cover.

As they travelled, John talked to Akimbo about crocodiles.

'If you're going to be helping me with my crocodiles,' he said, 'then you should know something about them.'

Akimbo was eager to learn and listened intently as John told him all about the life of the strange reptiles.

'They're just like any other animal,' he explained. 'Much of their life is spent looking for food and keeping warm.'

'So that's why they sunbathe,' Akimbo said. He had seen crocodiles resting on sandbanks, soaking up the warmth of the sun like sunbathers on a beach.

John nodded.

'They're cold-blooded,' he said. 'They have to store up heat from the sun. That's why they lie so still. They don't want to waste any energy.'

There were other things too. John told

him how the crocodile grabbed its prey, seizing it in its great jaws and then twisting it round to tear off the flesh.

'They have terrific power in their jaws,' he said. 'But it's all directed to snapping the jaws closed. The muscles that open the mouth are much weaker.'

Akimbo was fascinated. He had not realised that there was so much to learn about crocodiles, and he could hardly wait to get to the river so that they could start their search.

They stopped some distance short of the river itself.

'I don't want to disturb them,' John explained. 'We should walk from here, and keep our voices down as well. That way, if there are any crocodiles basking we should be able to spot them.'

They parked the truck under some trees to keep it cool. Then, being as quiet as he could, John led Akimbo through the thick scrub that lay between them and the edge of the river. Akimbo took great care where he put his feet – his father had taught him that this was the secret of moving silently through the bush. There were always twigs or small branches that would crack loudly if you trod on them.

The river at that point was fairly wide and moved slowly and sluggishly past reed-lined banks. Here and there, the surface of the water was broken by rocks, which jutted

out like small islands along a coast. There were also sandbanks, spits of golden brown sand that dipped below the green surface of the water. These were ideal places for crocodiles to bask, as they offered all that they needed – warmth, a good view of what was happening on the river banks, and an easy way back into the water if danger presented itself.

John crouched down and signalled to Akimbo to do the same. They were still a little way from the edge of the river, but they had good cover, as well as an uninterrupted view of several sandbanks and places where the river widened out into deep, still pools.

'This is an ideal place for them,' John whispered. 'If we stay here for a while we're bound to see something.'

Akimbo settled down on the ground beside the crocodile man and watched the river in front of him. The water looked so smooth and peaceful that it was difficult to imagine anything as dangerous as a crocodile lurking below it. In fact, as he sat there, he thought how nice and cool it would be to swim! Yet he had only to glance at John's scarred arm to remind himself that swimming was not a good idea.

For a long time nothing seemed to happen. Akimbo began to wonder whether they would ever see anything, but John seemed to be quite happy to sit patiently, watching the river, chewing at a blade of succulent green river grass which he had plucked.

Akimbo's attention had wandered, and he was looking at a group of chattering birds in a tree top when he felt John tug at his sleeve.

'There!' he said quietly. 'On the other side!'

Akimbo looked in the direction in which John was pointing. On the other side of the river, a few paces away from a sandbank, a dark object was moving slowly across the surface of the water.

'Two of them,' John whispered. 'The other one's slightly behind.'

Akimbo had to search for a while, but at last he picked out the snout of the second crocodile.

A few seconds later, the two crocodiles

had reached the sand bar and had begun to lumber up out of the water. As they did so, Akimbo drew in his breath.

'Yes,' whispered John. 'They're beauties. At least five metres each.'

Akimbo had never seen such large crocodiles and could hardly believe that they had been there all along, lurking somewhere in the pools or reeds. He and John watched silently as the two giant reptiles settled themselves on the bank. After a few minutes, the crocodiles became quite immobile, their giant heads resting in the warm sand, their tails stretched out behind them.

'They're not going to be doing very much today,' John said, rising to his feet. 'I think that we can have a quick look round and then go home.'

Akimbo and John both rose to their feet and made their way silently away from the bank. John led, picking his way with great caution, avoiding clumps of reed which were too dense to pass through, and taking care not to get too close to the water.

After a while, the reeds opened up before them and they found themselves on the edge of a broad sandbank. They stopped, making sure that there were no crocodiles on it, and then John went forwards, followed by Akimbo.

Akimbo was not sure what John was looking for, but whatever it was, he soon found it.

'Look down

there,' John said, pointing at the sand before him. 'That's what we're after.'

Akimbo looked down at the moist sand. There at their feet was a small mound, with some marks in the sand beside it, as if the surface had been scratched by some creature. But there was no other clue as to what it was.

'A crocodile nest,' said John, glancing over his shoulder towards the river. 'If you've never seen a crocodile's egg, then you're going to see one now!'

Catching a crocodile!

Gently, like a man uncovering a precious treasure, John brushed away the sand from the top of the nest. The covering was not thick, and soon Akimbo saw the first white of the shells revealed.

John lifted up one of the eggs, cupping it carefully in his hands. He tapped at it softly and held it up to the sun. Then he put it to his ear and shook it.

'There's a young crocodile in there,' he said. 'And it's only a few days from hatching.'

Akimbo watched as John put the egg back in place and softly covered the nest with sand again. After a minute or two the nest had been returned to exactly the state in which it had been found and nobody would have known that it had ever been disturbed.

John stood up and dusted the sand off his hands.

'Good,' he said. 'I think that's our day's work done. We'll come back here tomorrow, set up our observation post, and watch the young fellows hatch. Then we'll try to tag them, and the mother too. That way we'll be able to keep a record of the whole family.'

Akimbo followed John back to the truck, his mind seething with excitement.He wondered if the mother would be one of the massive crocodiles he had seen basking on the sandbank down river. It would be easy enough to tag the baby crocodiles, he imagined, but to tag the mother would certainly not be a simple task.

They reached home late that night. Akimbo wanted to tell his father all about their day, but he was just too exhausted. The next morning, though, over breakfast he recounted what they had done and took great pleasure in describing the full size of the two basking crocodiles.

'I don't like the sound of that,' Akimbo's father said. 'Are you sure that you want to carry on with this?'

Akimbo nodded.

'And there's a nest too,' he said. 'We're going to watch the young ones hatch.'

They set off later that day. Four men from the ranger station came with them, and in the back of the truck there was heaped what seemed to Akimbo to be a mountain of supplies. There were tents, nets, thick ropes, and several other specialised pieces of equipment which Akimbo did not recognize.

When they reached the river, they had to make several trips by foot, carrying the equipment from the truck to the place near the sandbank where they had located the nest. It was hard work in the heat, but at last everything was piled up in one place and could be sorted out.

First of all, two tents were erected in a place which gave a view of the sandbank. Then, after John had checked the bank itself, the nets and ropes were carried down to the thick clump of reeds that grew about the edges of the bank. The nets were unwound and put in a position where they could be picked up quickly, and the same was done for the ropes.

After an hour or so, John appeared satisfied with the preparations. He called the men around him and gave each one his instructions. Akimbo was to stay in the tent, he said, when they were using the nets. But at least he could help with the tagging of the little crocodiles.

'Their teeth are pretty small,' John said. 'They can't give you much more than a nip.'

With everything in place, they made their way back to the tents and sat inside them, grateful for the shade. Now there was nothing to do but to sit and wait.

* * *

It was one of the men who saw the crocodile first. He whispered to John, who looked out and nodded. Akimbo peered out from the mouth of the tent and saw the black shape at the edge of the sandbank, just below the surface of the water. He could tell that it was a crocodile, and a large one at that.

Now John and the men crept out of the tent and soon disappeared into the bank of reeds. Akimbo watched, his heart thumping with excitement, as the crocodile moved up on to the sandbank. She stopped near the nest and seemed to stay quite still, as if she were guarding it. It must be the mother, thought Akimbo. Had she sensed that somebody had disturbed the nest?

For a few minutes nothing happened. Then Akimbo saw the reeds at the far end of the bank move. He saw the heads of two of the men, and he thought he spotted a piece of net. Then, on the other side of the bank, John's head appeared. Akimbo held his breath. Whatever was going to happen would surely happen soon.

There was a sudden shout, and Akimbo saw the crocodile lurch round and make a dash for the water's edge. It would take her no more than a few seconds to be back in her element, but that was enough time for John to dart across the sand, dragging one of the nets behind him.

The crocodile continued her plunge, but

it was too late, and she lunged headlong into the net. As she did so, two more of the men came out and threw the folds of another net over the struggling beast.

It seemed to Akimbo as if the whole sandbank had erupted into movement. The crocodile turned and thrashed with her tail, but all that she did was to enmesh herself more firmly in the net. It was impossible for her to escape.

Now John came with a rope, and began to loop it round the crocodile's tail. Then more rope was brought, and soon the whole struggling mixture of beast and net was firmly trussed in straining coils of rope.

John looked up and beckoned to Akimbo.

'It's safe now,' he called. 'She can't do much like this.'

Akimbo ran down to the sandbank and stood beside John as they examined their still writhing, but helpless captive. A rope had been wound round her jaws and she could not open them. Her tail, too, had been secured, although it still twisted and battled against the restraint.

'We'll waste no time,' said John. 'We don't want to harm her.'

With that, he picked up a curious implement which had been laid to one side. This was the tagging device, and John quickly snipped a metal tag between its jaws. Then, approaching the crocodile carefully, he selected one of the bumps along the top of its tail, and clipped the tag into the skin.

'Won't that hurt her?' Akimbo asked.

'She won't feel a thing,' John reassured him. 'But she's marked from now on.'

John left the crocodile's side.

'Now,' he said. 'Here comes the difficult part. Akimbo, you stand back while we let her free.'

It was not simple disentangling an angry crocodile, but at last the final fold of net was dragged away and the reptile found herself free. With a great hissing sound, she shot away, plunging into the river with a splash.

John signalled to the men to leave, and together they all abandoned the bank and clambered back up to the tent.

'Now we have to wait for the hatching,' John explained to Akimbo. 'And that's going to be fun.'

The baby
crocodiles arrive

They had brought enough provisions for four days. John thought that the eggs were due to hatch soon, but he could not be certain.

'There's nothing to do but wait,' he said. 'They'll hatch sooner or later.'

They did not hatch that day, nor that night. At night time, every two hours one of the men crept down to the sandbank to see if anything had happened. Each time the report was the same: the mound of sand was undisturbed.

At first Akimbo tried to keep awake, so that he would not miss any of the excitement, but John assured him that he would arouse him if anything happened. When Akimbo awoke the next morning, with the first rays of the sun streaming in through the mouth of the tent, one of the men was just returning from the sandbank.

'Nothing,' he said, shaking his head. 'Nothing at all.'

The watch continued. At mid-morning they drank tea, brewed by one of the men, and at midday they had lunch. Then, as the pots which the men had used to cook the maize meal were being packed away, John gave a low whistle.

'All right, everyone,' he said. 'Things are beginning to happen.'

They made their way down to the

sandbank as quickly as they could, but even though they hurried they missed the first of the newly-hatched crocodiles. Part of the sand covering of the nest had been scraped away, and the top of a shattered and empty egg was exposed to the sun.

They stood around the nest, watching the miracle that was being performed before their very eyes. The next egg was breaking now, cracking across the top to reveal a struggling, slimy creature within. Then a snout appeared, the tip of a tail, and within moments a complete and perfect tiny crocodile had scurried out on to the sand.

John reached forwards and plucked the midget creature from the ground. Then, expertly closing the tiny, snapping jaws, he applied a small shining tag to the tail. It took no more than a few seconds, after which the little creature was dropped back on the sand to scurry off towards the water.

The rest followed smoothly. The eggs were all now exposed, and over the next hour or so almost all of them cracked open and hatched a tiny crocodile. Each was tagged and pointed down towards the water. Each disappeared into the river within seconds. Only a few eggs, which John said were infertile, did not open. These were carefully packed away for further examination.

As John performed his work, two of the men kept watch at the end of the sandbank.

'The mother will be around here somewhere,' John said. 'But she probably won't dare come out. There are rather too many of us for her.'

When all the baby crocodiles had been tagged, John, who had counted each one, made an entry in a book and gathered up his equipment. It was now time to go, to pack up the tent and leave the crocodiles in peace – at least for the time being.

'We can come back tomorrow,' John said to Akimbo. 'If we look very carefully we might be able to spot these youngsters around at the edge of the river. Would you like that?'

Akimbo said that he would. It had been a most extraordinary sight seeing the tiny crocodiles emerging into the world, and he hoped with all his heart that they would be alive the next day. John had explained to him that there were all sorts of dangers to be faced by crocodiles in their first few days. They could even be eaten by large birds, he said; a heron could pick up and swallow a newly-hatched crocodile just as it would swallow a fish.

'Their mother will be able to protect them some of the time,' he went on. 'Do you know that she shelters her young inside her jaws for the first few days?'

Akimbo found it hard to imagine. If he were looking for shelter, he thought that the inside of a crocodile's mouth would be the very last place he would try!

Crocodile attack

They returned to the river the next day without any of the men from the ranger station. It would be better for them to go alone, said John, as the presence of more people just meant more disturbance and less chance of seeing crocodiles. Besides, John planned to launch his inflatable boat on the river, and this really only had room for two.

Akimbo was excited at the prospect of going in the boat, and he was even more thrilled when John said he could start off rowing it.

'Take it gently,' said John. 'We're in no hurry, and the last thing we want to do is land up in the water!'

They eased the small boat into the river and then, while John held the bow, Akimbo waded out as deep as his

knees and climbed aboard. John followed him and then pushed away from the shore with one of the metal oars. Soon the gentle current of the river had picked them up and begun to carry them downstream.

Akimbo found rowing harder than he had imagined, but soon mastered it and had them moving slowly up river against the current. They stayed out in the middle, well away from any rocks or shallows, and watched the reed banks move slowly past.

By the time they were nearing the sandbank where the hatching had taken place, Akimbo's arms were tired of rowing and he willingly handed the oars over to John.

John dipped the blades into the water so gently that there was hardly a ripple. He was watching the edge of the water intently now, and suddenly he gestured sharply to Akimbo.

'That's them,' he whispered, pointing towards a reedy part of the bank.

Akimbo stared at the water's edge, but could see nothing. Then he noticed a little movement, and then another. In the meantime, John had turned the boat and was slowly approaching the edge. As the boat drifted into the reeds, he handed the paddle to Akimbo and then, without warning, his hand darted out and plucked a glistening little crocodile out of the water.

He held the little creature out towards Akimbo and pointed to its tail. There was the tag, still in position, identifying it as one of theirs.

'He's made it to his second day,' John said, laughing as

he dropped the tiny crocodile back into the water. 'Good luck!'

They found three more shortly after that, and then John took the paddle again and

propelled the boat out into the middle of the river. Then they made their way further upstream, travelling quietly, as John hoped to see other crocodiles on sandbanks further up. But the river bank seemed deserted for the time being, although Akimbo knew well that this did not mean that there were no crocodiles about.

* * *

They had negotiated several bends in the river when they came across the island. It was at a point where the river broadened out considerably and was fairly shallow in parts. The island was not big, but supported a fair amount of vegetation, including a clump of tall, heavy-leafed trees. John was delighted to have found it, and quickly paddled the boat over to a muddy beach about half-way along one side.

They beached the boat and got out to explore. John wanted to see if there were any sandy places which might be used by crocodiles for hatching. Akimbo wanted to walk from one end to the other, just to see what it was like.

'Be careful of snakes,' John warned as Akimbo made his way up to the ridge that ran through the middle of the island. 'Have a look round, and then come back here.'

Akimbo climbed up to the top of the ridge and looked down. John had left the boat on the muddy beach and was making his way through the reeds, looking for signs of crocodiles.

Akimbo turned away and began his exploration of the island. There was not much to see, though. There were no animals, although he thought he saw monkeys in a tree at one point, and there were no interesting rocks or caves. All in all, he thought, as he reached the tip of the island and turned back, it's a boring place.

It was then that he heard the cry. It was a shout, a yell, and it came from the other end of the island. Akimbo stopped in his tracks and listened, but all he heard was the screeching of cicadas and the sound of calling birds. Then there was another cry, and this time Akimbo knew.

Running wildly, blindly, his heart pumping fear into his limbs, Akimbo crashed through the undergrowth. It took him only a few minutes, and he was there, at the point of the ridge from which he had set out. And there below him, he saw John, half in the water and half out, struggling and calling out in a mass of foaming water.

Akimbo jumped, half fell down the ridge, and reached out to grab his friend. He knew what was happening, but had little idea how to help.

'The paddle!' shouted John. 'Get the paddle!'

Akimbo spun round and reached for the paddle which lay beside the boat. In an instant, he noticed that the boat had been ripped, and was now a deflated piece of limp rubber.

Akimbo seized the paddle, raised it in the air, and brought it down with all his strength on a twisting dark shape that seemed to have attached itself to John's leg. There was a dull thud, and the shock of contact. Akimbo raised the paddle once more and brought it down again with all his force.

At the second blow, the dark shape seemed to lurch backward, and then, in a froth of foam and churning water, was gone. The river calmed, and Akimbo saw John stagger out of the shallows where he had been struggling with his attacker. Safely back on the mud bank, he slumped backwards and pulled himself the last few inches out of the water.

Akimbo knelt beside his friend. He looked at his leg, and saw that it had been terribly bitten. Bright red blood streaked down, staining the mud beside the injured limb. Without hesitation, Akimbo slipped off his shirt and bound it quickly round the wound, making it as tight as he could in an effort to staunch the flow of blood.

'Thank you,' said John, his voice thick and shaky. 'You came just in time.'

The bandage seemed to be having its effect and the flow of blood slowed down to a trickle. John tried to stand, but the injured leg would not support him and he fell back against the mud.

'It's no use,' he said. 'I think a bone's broken.'

Akimbo glanced at the boat, and John shook his head sadly.

'He attacked me just as I was trying to launch it,' he said. 'I was going to come round to the other end to pick you up there. He got me as I pulled it out.'

Akimbo looked at John's wounded leg again. He would have to get help soon, as the bleeding had not stopped altogether and there was a limit to the amount of blood that could be lost. And yet, with the boat destroyed, there seemed to be no way of getting that help. Could they just wait it out? How long would it be before a search party found them? It could be a day or two, or even more. And if it took that long, would John survive his terrible injury which the crocodile had inflicted on him?

Akimbo thought not. He would have to go for help himself. There was no other way.

A dangerous swim

'I'll swim across,' said Akimbo. 'Then I'll go down river until I get to the truck. I'm sure I can drive it.'

John shook his head.

'You can't go into that water,' he said firmly. 'You wouldn't make it. There are too many crocodiles around here.'

'I could swim quickly,' said Akimbo. 'I'm a strong swimmer.'

John raised his voice, half in pain, half to show Akimbo that he meant it when he told him not to do it.

'No,' he said. 'You can't. You wouldn't make it.'

Akimbo looked out at the river. Perhaps there was a place where it was shallow enough to wade across; perhaps there was a place with stones. But the river, although not always deep, was not that shallow. The only way of crossing was to swim, or . . . Akimbo smiled. Yes. He had remembered the fallen branch which he had seen just a little way up the ridge. He had had to step over it, and he had thought how it could well have made a dug-out canoe.

He turned to John and explained his plan enthusiastically. He could roll the branch down to the bank and launch it from there. It might not be the perfect boat, but at least it would float. The paddle had survived the encounter with the crocodile, and he could use that to propel the log across to the other side.

John seemed doubtful.

'You're still going to have your legs in the water,' he said. 'And the log might not be so easy to steer. You could find yourself floating downstream for hours.'

'It's not that big,' argued Akimbo. 'I'm sure I'll manage.'

He looked at John's injured leg. Blood was still seeping through the bandage.

'I've got to get help,' Akimbo said. 'There's no other way.'

John gave a wince of pain. He knew that Akimbo was right, and so at last he nodded his reluctant agreement to the plan.

Akimbo did not waste time. Scampering up to the top of the ridge, he found the fallen

branch and roughly manhandled it down to the bank. It was hard work, and the bark of the branch was rough on his hands, but eventually he managed to move it into position and the log was floating, half-submerged, at the edge of the river.

Akimbo made sure that John was as comfortable as possible. Then, picking up the paddle, he waded out gingerly and clambered up on to his improvised boat.

John had been right about paddling a log. It was much more difficult than Akimbo had imagined, and for the first few minutes

Akimbo's efforts seemed to make no impression on the floating branch. Then slowly it began to respond, and the boy and his unusual boat began to edge out into the broad stream of the river.

To begin with, Akimbo did not have enough time to think about the danger he was in. All his attention was focused on remaining upright, as the branch seemed to want to roll with the current. If I fall in, he thought, that's the end.

He tried not to think of the giant crocodiles they had seen on the sandbank a few days previously. He tried particularly hard not to think of what might be below him in the water at that very moment. But it was impossible not to be afraid, and Akimbo was as frightened then as he had ever been in his life.

After a few minutes the log was in midstream. There was a stronger current now, and Akimbo felt the log begin to turn its bow down river. He paddled harder, in an attempt to direct it towards the bank, but this only made it dip and buck against him. He stopped paddling for a moment and the movement stopped.

Then, quite without warning, the log twisted strongly to one side. It might have been something that Akimbo did, or it might have struck a submerged obstacle, but the movement took Akimbo by surprise and he felt his balance going. He pulled the paddle over to the other side in a frantic attempt to stay upright, but it was too late and he felt himself toppling.

Akimbo entered the water with a splash, feeling its treacherous embrace all about him. Relieved of his weight, the log reared up in the water and moved off swiftly with the current.

Akimbo struggled upwards to the surface. He had lost the log, and he had lost the paddle, and in a terrible moment of understanding he felt himself completely alone in the crocodile-infested water.

Instinctively he struck out for the shore, battling desperately to quell the panic within him. He tried to swim as quietly as possible, moving his hands through the water without splashing. He knew that any unusual sound or movement could attract crocodiles, and so his best chance was to move through the water as smoothly as he could.

Something brushed against Akimbo's leg, and for an instant he froze, sinking in terror. But nothing else happened, and it could have been anything – a fish, a piece of weed, a sunken branch. He started to swim again, although the river's edge seemed as far away as ever.

Suddenly Akimbo felt ground beneath his feet. It was soft, slippery mud, but it made his heart soar. He lunged forwards, half-swimming, half-walking, and was soon out of the water, hardly believing that he had made it to safety.

For a few minutes he sat on the bank and rested, recovering his strength. Then, rising to his feet, he began the journey back to the place where the truck had been parked.

Getting help

Akimbo started off on his journey, running as fast as he could through the thick bush. Sharp branches whipped at him as he ran past; thorns tore at his skin; but he felt nothing. His heart pumping wildly within him, he pushed himself to go faster, ignoring the stitch that had begun to needle at his side. But at last he could run no more, and he slowed down and rested. Looking back, it seemed to him as if he had travelled hardly any distance at all.

'It's easy in a boat,' he said to himself. 'It takes five times longer on foot.'

He stood for a few minutes, gulping in the air, waiting to get his breath back. Then, his heart beating less wildly, he began to trot off again, keeping the bank of the river just within sight, but avoiding the thick reed beds that lined the water's edge. His feet were sore, as one of his shoes had lost part of its sole, and was pinching him at each step. He tried to put most of his weight on his other leg, but this just slowed him down even more. So, bending down to undo his laces, he pulled off both shoes and went ahead barefoot.

For almost an hour, Akimbo fought his way through the heavy bush, until at last, just when he was beginning to think that he might never reach it, he saw in the distance the clump of trees where the truck was parked. He put on an extra spurt of speed now, leaping over the narrow, overgrown ditches that cut across the land, paying no attention to the sharp stones that dug into the soles of his feet.

'I'll make it after all,' he muttered to himself. 'I'll save you, John!'

The truck was half in the shade, half in the sun, and as a result it had become boiling hot. As Akimbo opened the door of the cab, a solid wall of heat came out to greet him. He slid into the cab, and pulled the door closed behind him. Then he reached forwards to start the engine.

It was at this point that he made an awful discovery. There was no key. For a moment, his mind went blank. Why had he not thought about it? How could he have been so stupid? The key, of course, was probably in John's pocket – why had he not thought to ask him for it? John had no doubt realised this already. Perhaps he had called out to him after he had left, to remind him, and he had not heard.

Akimbo leaned forwards, his eyes filling with tears. He would never rescue John now. If he ran all the way back – which would take him much longer now that he was tired – he would have to come all the way back again. And then it would probably be too late to save John, and it would all be his fault for forgetting something as simple as the key of the truck.

Just as he was thinking this, an image came into Akimbo's mind. It was his father talking to him, telling him what he had told him once before when they had both been faced with a problem which seemed insoluble.

'Never give up,' his father had said. 'Think of other ways of doing what you have to do. You'll be surprised at how often that works!'

Akimbo could almost hear his father's voice. *Think of other ways of doing what you have to do.* Yes! There was another way, but would he be able to do it? Akimbo was very uncertain, but at least he could try.

Akimbo remembered that he had once before seen one of his father's assistants start a truck without the key. He had watched carefully, as it had interested him, and he had thought at the time that it was really rather easy. The man had taken a short length of wire and connected two points behind the ignition. Then, after he had bridged two other points, the engine had swung into life, as if by magic. He had explained it carefully to Akimbo, and pointed out just where the wires must touch. But would he remember it?

It was not difficult to find two short pieces of wire in the tool box which the truck carried. Then, getting down on his hands

and knees, Akimbo peered under the dashboard. It was a maze of wires, but he was soon able to see just where the key slotted into the ignition and to make out the points which must be bridged.

Gingerly, willing his hands not to shake, Akimbo moved the two ends of one of the pieces of wire into position. There was a clicking sound, and he noticed a bulb behind the instrument panel grow red. That was the first step, and he had done it correctly. Now he reached for the other pieces of wire and very carefully bridged the point between the two ends of what he thought must be the starter switch.

As the wire touched the contacts, Akimbo let out a scream. A powerful current of electricity shot into his fingers and his hand and snaked its way up his arm. As it did so, the engine leapt into life and, to Akimbo's horror, the truck lurched forwards. In his eagerness to get the truck started, Akimbo had forgotten to check that the gears were disengaged. Now he had started the truck, just as he wanted to, but he was on the floor, and the steering wheel was spinning round as the truck began to career off.

Akimbo struggled to pull himself up. The movement of the truck did not help, but at

last he managed to wrench himself up on to the seat and grab the steering wheel. The truck had built up some speed in the short time that it had been running, and Akimbo saw, looming before them, the shape of a large tree. He was sure that it was too late, that they would collide with the tree, and he inadvertently closed his eyes as he wrenched at the wheel and sought to bring that charging truck away from its course.

There was no sickening thud. There was no sound of crumpling metal. Akimbo opened his eyes, and saw that they had just

missed the large tree and that they were bumping harmlessly over an open patch of grass. Now he pushed in the clutch, changed to a lower gear, and felt the large machine respond to his control. Slowly he swung the wheel round, bringing the truck into the direction he wanted it to follow. It did just as he asked it, and for the first time since the disappointment of finding that he had no key, Akimbo began to feel optimistic about his chances of saving John.

At last Akimbo found his way back on to one of the major tracks that led to the ranger camp. He set off down this, driving as fast as he dared, hoping that when he arrived at the camp his father would be there. He imagined John lying on the island, his leg throbbing with pain. He imagined the crocodiles, watching perhaps from the shadows, waiting for their victim to weaken to the point where he would be easy prey. There was no time to lose.

He had only been driving for ten minutes or so when he saw one of the other ranger trucks coming fast towards him. It seemed almost too good to be true, but Akimbo pulled in, disengaged the gears, and applied the brake. Then, as the other truck drew level with him and stopped, its surprised driver leant out of his window and called out.

'Akimbo! What on earth are you up to?'

Akimbo explained as quickly as he could. Then, leaving his truck by the side of the track, he leapt into the other vehicle and the driver put everything he could into getting them to the river bank in less than half an hour. Fortunately, he had been making his way to another part of the river, and there was another inflatable boat in the back. This they launched in record time, and they found John half-sitting, half-lying at the top of a bank, his injured leg straight out before him.

Akimbo could tell that John was in pain, but in spite of this he still seemed cheerful.

'That was quick,' said John. 'I was all set for a much longer wait.'

'I was worried that the crocodiles would get you,' Akimbo said. 'Did you see them?'

'No,' said John. 'But they were there all right. I think that they were, well, I think that they were *interested*!'

They soon had John in the boat and they made the short crossing to the other side.

Then Akimbo helped to carry the injured man to the truck where he was laid out on some empty sacks. After that, there was the rapid drive to the hospital, which was almost fifty miles away. John bumped about rather a lot in the back of the truck, but did not complain. He even managed to smile as Akimbo told him all about the way he had started the truck without the key.

'I didn't even think of it,' said John. 'It's just as well you're a mechanic!'

They watched John being wheeled into the small bush hospital.

'There's no point in waiting,' said the ranger who had driven them there. 'They'll

let us know how things go. I'm sure that everything will be all right!'

And he was right. The next day they received a telephone call from the doctor to announce that all was well.

'The bandage stopped the bleeding,' he said. 'Without it I don't think he would have made it.'

Three days later, Akimbo's father took him to the small bush hospital to visit John. He found him in a little room, propped up against several thick pillows, writing in a notebook.

'So!' said John, laying aside the book. 'My rescuer!'

Akimbo smiled modestly.

'It wasn't hard,' he said. 'The only time I was afraid was when I fell in.'

John nodded. 'I'm glad I didn't see that,'

he said. 'That place was itching with crocs.'

'Perhaps they weren't hungry,' said Akimbo.

'Or perhaps they didn't like the taste of me,' joked John. 'That might have put them off for a while.'

They talked for a time, until John asked Akimbo to fetch a parcel which was sitting on the table on the other side of the room.

'Open it,' he said. 'It's for you. It's a little present for what you did.'

Akimbo unwrapped the parcel and found himself holding a large book. There, on the cover, was a picture of a crocodile on a bank, and there was John's name in large, black print. It was John's book on crocodiles, the book Akimbo had so wanted to read.

Akimbo opened the book. On the first page, written boldly in ink, was the inscription: 'For Akimbo. Thank you.' And beneath it was John's signature.

'You may have had enough of crocodiles for the time being,' said John. 'But maybe you'll read it some day.'

'I'll start straight away,' said Akimbo.

John mused for a moment.

'Next year,' he said, 'when I come back to check up on that family in the river, will you give me a hand?'

'Of course,' said Akimbo. 'I'll be there.'

John looked pleased.

'I think we'll make a crocodile man out of you one of these days,' he said, laughing as he spoke.

'I'd like that,' said Akimbo. 'I really would.'